BETWEEN SEA AND SAND

THE SELKI SISTERS

BOOK TWO

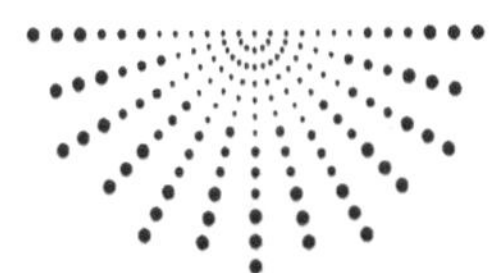

SHARON BRUBAKER

ACKNOWLEDGMENTS

This book could not be written without my 'boots on the ground' person in Long Island. Many heartfelt thanks to Holly L'Hommedieu of HL Sea and Beach Glass Jewelry

https://www.hlseabeachglassjewelry.com/

For Rob – another love letter.

Many thanks to my family for their love and support in writing each book.

Thank you, Alice Lundgren, for the friendship, sanity, support, and beta reading.

Thank you to Melissa Feliciano for teaching me about "The Light."

Many thanks to Nicole Maggi, editor extraordinaire.

Many thanks to Nicole Scarano for formatting.

Many thanks to Faera Lane for the lovely book cover.

And thank you to Sarah Detmer for Writing Camp and beta listening.

A portion of the Selki Series sales will be donated to the Marine Mammal Stranding Center, Brigantine, New Jersey (mmsc.org). Thank you for all you do for marine mammals!

I am the sea
You are the earth.
I am the wave.
You are my shore.

1

MAURA

$\mathcal{M}$aura struggled. Her body did not want to cooperate, and her lungs felt like lead weights. Breaking through the water's surface, the cool air rushed toward her. She tried to take a large breath, but coughs wracked her body, causing her to slip beneath the waves and bring water into her lungs.

Again, she fought to reach the air. Spluttering, she moved torpidly through the water, chest heaving, to reach the shoreline. It was exhausting. Eventually, she caught the swells' rhythm, and they gently pushed her along. Her eyes rested on the prize – the soft, sandy shore. She was getting closer and closer in infinitesimal amounts. She let the water lift her until she reached the breakers, which pushed her the rest of the way. She landed hard on the beach, waves crashing. Water coursed around her, the tide trying to pull her back into the ocean. Maura knew she had to move further up the beach.

Her breathing had been so labored with the virus she had caught. She thought she might die like so many others. Deep in her heart, she knew the sea took care of itself. She wouldn't die. It was as if the sea was a supporting hug, wrapping its arms around her, embracing her towards the shore. She inched forward, using her stomach muscles to help her move on the land, her rear flippers held up in the air behind her. Maura pushed herself until she reached the tideline, where the sea met the shore, leaving a decorative ruffle of shells, stones, and seaweed. She lay, heaving breath by heaving breath, for several moments. After what seemed like hours, she worked to peel off her pelt. Once away from the water, Maura used her front flippers to tug and pull the head of her pelt back, allowing cold air to rush past her face. A bit of it made it into her lungs. It was cold. It burned. But it was so, so good.

Bit by bit, she pulled the pelt from her body and her flippers. She lay on the sand, exhausted from the effort, her skin bright pink, as if scrubbed clean. The air on her body caused her to shake with cold. Her body raged with fever. She drew her pelt over her like a blanket. It was heavy and wet but was the only thing to help assuage the bone-chilling cold.

She looked up at the sky. The clouds scudded across the moon, snuffing out stars as they passed. Were these her last moments on this earth? Her vision grew cloudy. The ocean roared in her ears, and Maura sank into fevered oblivion.

2

RORY

Rory cried out with an "oof!" and flailed his arms when two large, black paws landed on his chest, waking him from a sound sleep. Scratchy whiskers, foul dog breath, and a large, slimy tongue licking his face from chin to crown erased the dream he was having.

The large black lab mix pawed at Rory's chest. Rory gently grabbed his ears and vigorously rubbed them. The dog gave a low moan of pleasure and leaned into Rory's hands.

"Good morning to you, Skipper," Rory told the dog.

The dog pushed off his chest and danced around the bedroom, nose to the ground, seeking something. He sneezed when he snuffled under the bed and used a paw to draw out a ball. Skipper took the ball, jumped on the bed, and dropped the ball on top of Rory.

"Okay, okay, I get the picture. But it would help if you got off the bed so that I can get up," he told the dog, laughing at the dog's insistence on playing.

Rory tossed the ball across the room, and Skipper flew off the bed to fetch it. He took the opportunity to get out of bed quickly, pull on his jeans, and layer a sweatshirt and hoodie over his sleep t-shirt. He shoved his feet into boots.

"Let me make a quick cup of coffee.

Skipper shot out of the bedroom and waited anxiously by the kitchen door, ball in his mouth, tail wagging vigorously while Rory made coffee. He donned a warm beanie and juggled his coffee, dog leash, and waste bags in one arm while he worked to unlock and open the door with the other.

Skipper pushed his nose into the door, forcing it to open further before he raced outside and bolted down the steps to the beach. Rory laughed at his dog's antics, stepped onto his deck, and stood momentarily, taking in the view.

The ocean and sky glowed in the pearly, early morning light. The clouds hung as if suspended on invisible threads. Rory took a deep breath of the salty air, relishing the day's quiet. That was, until Skipper barked at the bottom of the stairs, urging Rory to come to the beach.

Rory loved the solitude of his neighborhood. In November, the bulk of the residents had gone back to their winter homes. Occasionally, he would see a sea glasser or fisherman, but most of the time, this expanse of sea and sky was all his own during the winter months. He grinned, feeling like a king.

He stood at the bottom of the stairs and sipped coffee. Skipper was anxious for him to throw the ball and nudged it toward him, tail wagging. Rory picked up the ball and tossed it down the beach. Skipper raced after it. Rory meandered, the dog returning again and again as Rory threw the ball for him. The beach curved around the small cove where Rory's cottage sat. He threw the ball again. Skipper raced after it but did not return quickly as he usually did. Instead, he barked and barked. Puzzled, Rory picked up his step to investigate.

"What is it, boy?" Rory called out.

Ahead, he saw a heap of something in the sand. Skipper was a few feet back, barking over and over.

What was it? He approached warily. He called Skipper to him, telling him to sit.

"Good boy," he murmured and patted the dog's head. He gave the hand signal for Skipper to stay. The dog sat, practically dancing in his spot, but he obeyed, panting and not taking his eyes off the lump ahead.

Rory approached slowly. At first, he thought it was an animal. He knew enough to keep his distance from the seals that occasionally beached themselves to take a rest. But this was different. He saw pale legs attached to long feet and luxuriant, curly locks of dark hair.

Rory gulped a mouthful of hot coffee, burning his throat and gaping at the body on the beach. This was like something from a movie, definitely far from his usual reality. A body on the beach? He wondered if the body of the woman in front of him was alive or dead. She had something draped over her that looked like the pelt of a seal, complete with a head. It was the most elaborate cosplay he had ever seen. It looked like a real seal.

"Ma'am?" he called to her. "Ma'am? Are you all right?"

The lump didn't move. He went closer. She was naked beneath the costume, and her rosy nipples were erect as the cool November air washed over them. Long dark lashes fluttered, revealing the largest, darkest brown eyes he had ever seen. Fear. He saw fear in them.

"It's okay," he assured her. "I won't hurt you. Are you hurt?"

She was mute, still staring at him. She cringed, pressing her body into the sand in fear. She shot furtive glances as she eyed Skipper.

"That's Skipper, my dog. He won't hurt you either. He's a good dog. Is there someone I can call for you? Should I call 911?" He reached into his pocket and found it empty. He had forgotten to pick up his phone.

"Caite?" she asked, squinting in the bright morning light. Coughs wracked her entire body, and she gasped for air.

It sounded like, "Catch ya," to Rory. He didn't understand. But this woman was clearly ill. He got closer and saw that her skin was flushed with fever. She tried to talk again but coughed instead. The effort of coughing wore her out. Her eyelids fluttered, and she either fell asleep or passed out.

Rory wasn't sure what to do. His brain raced with wild thoughts of "what ifs" bringing a stranger home. What if she got the wrong impression when he brought her home? What if she was crazy? The animal skin on top of her made him draw back. It stank of dead fish and the sea. He felt lost without his phone. She obviously didn't have any identification, naked under that animal's skin. Who was she? Why was she here? But his second thought was that she obviously needed help. He couldn't let her lie on the beach. He scooped her up in his arms, pelt and all, and took her back to his house. Skipper trotted beside him, quiet now.

Rory took the woman into the guest bedroom, and as carefully as possible, he put her in the bed, pulling the covers around her and tucking her in. The pelt had fallen to the floor. Its briny, fishy scent filled the room. Rory picked it up and took it outside, unsure what to do. He wrinkled his nose at the strong scent. She must have been swimming in it. Occasionally, the wild swimmers came to his beach in all seasons, but he had never seen one in a costume. He shook his head in wonderment and looked around where he could put what appeared to be a seal costume. He didn't want to leave it on the back deck, even though it could use an airing. He spied the shed where he kept his yard tools and decided to take it there, draping it over a small garden cart. The empty eyes of the seal head and whiskers spooked him a little. He turned, locked the door, and returned to the house.

Skipper had settled in next to the woman, snuggling his warm body against her. She breathed shallowly and continued to sleep. Rory ran his fingers through his hair and tugged at his curls. Now what?

He went to get some water for the woman and another cup of coffee for himself. He sat in the small upholstered chair in the corner of the room and watched her. She was beautiful. Her long, curling dark hair splayed over the pillow, and he itched to run his hands through it. She had tiny, shell-like ears, almost miniature, and a petite nose that turned up with a heart shape at the end. It was adorable. The zaftig curves of her petite body showed through the bedclothes. He felt his jeans grow tight as his desire grew.

Skipper looked up at him with hooded eyes as if to say, "Are you kidding?"

"You're right, Skipper, this isn't the time," he said quietly.

Skipper thumped his tail softly and moved closer to the woman, laying his head on her legs. She sighed and continued to sleep.

3

MAURA

$\mathcal{M}$aura's fevered dreams were a jumble of images. She was swimming slowly through the water. Large strands of kelp seemed to wrap around her body and hold her tightly. She had to struggle to pull away from the strands, but they seemed to hold onto her more tightly the more she struggled. Later, she dreamed of a man. He had dark hair and worried blue eyes behind his glasses. Did she know him? She felt she did. There was something about him... And the dreams continued to swirl in her head. She thrashed about, trying to release herself from the kelp. She was burning hot and then freezing cold.

Finally, she dreamed she was on the beach with the rest of the seal pack. When it was cold, they moved together for warmth. Maura felt one of the seals lean against her, their large body pressed comfortingly next to hers. She sighed, finally feeling comforted, and slept deeply.

Hours later, she woke discombobulated. She realized immediately she wasn't in the ocean or on the beach. Where was she? The texture of what she was cocooned in was soft and comfortable but different from the feel of sand or water.

She looked, her eyes traveling around the room. Above her was a snowy white ceiling. The walls of the room were a deep, blue-grey, not unlike a stormy ocean.

Then, she looked down at her legs, heavy with the weight of something. It was the beast – a dog. Frightened, she grasped the bedclothes and quickly pulled them to her chin for protection. But this dog wasn't barking. Instead, his tail thumped in a friendly manner. His eyes looked at her expectantly. They were deep eyes as if they held the soul of the world and were friendly. They didn't have the "I'm going to eat you" look that the eyes of predators had. Its tail thumped again. Tentatively, she took her hand and arm from beneath the covers and stretched it towards the dog. He gave her fingers a lick with a soft, wet tongue. It felt odd but strangely comforting as the dog licked her fingers. She drew back.

Her eyes fell next to the man, asleep in a chair near the bed. His mouth was hanging slightly open, and his whiskers had grown to make shadows on his face. His curly, dark hair was mussed, and his glasses were askew on his face. His lanky form looked as bunched up on the small chair and stool as his crumpled clothes. He was tall, with large hands and long fingers, his palms lying against his body. He slept soundly and snored lightly. Maura put her hand to her mouth to suppress a giggle. He reminded her of a bull seal asleep on the beach.

There was something about him. She didn't know if it was his presence or essence, but she was attracted to him. A fire stirred in her belly and between her legs. She squirmed a little, disturbing the dog, who protested with a low moan before he rearranged himself on her. She was surprised by the emotions and desire. She had never felt like this about a bull seal. In fact, they repelled her, and she had spent the better part of this last year fending them off. These emotions and desires were entirely new.

But where was her pelt? She looked wildly, then, about the room. It was nowhere to be seen. Did the man take it? Was it lying on the beach or lost to the sea? If the man took it…her eyes narrowed now, looking at him, wondering. Her gran and her mum had told her stories of men who did this, locking up a Selki's pelt and keeping the woman a prisoner. Her sister, Celine, had been taken prisoner by a human. He kept her pelt. He raped her. He abused her. She pined for the sea and eventually died. Since then, she had a distrust for humans – particularly men.

Hurt and anger were buried beneath an overwhelming fear of this man. She didn't think she could trust him or any man. She began to cough again. The man jumped, startled at the sound, and opened his eyes.

"You're awake," he commented, reaching for a glass of water by the bed and thrusting it into her hand. "Here, this should help."

Initially hesitant, Maura took the glass trepidatiously and drank the water, hoping it would quell her cough. The water was so clear and sweet, with only the faintest tinge of brine. She drank it greedily.

"Easy now," the man said. "Take it easy, or you'll get a stomach ache."

She stopped drinking and looked at him. This time, she was astonished by his kindness. And she stared; his eyes were clear, bluish-green, almost the color of a southern sea. They were slightly muted behind his round glasses rimmed in black, but they looked at her with kindness and concern.

Her cough, momentarily silent, Maura greeted him, "Latha math."

He looked at her, puzzled.

"Good day," she tried again, this time in English.

"Hello." He smiled briefly. "How are you feeling?"

Maura considered this question. She was much better than she had been in the last few days. Her chest didn't feel as heavy as before, though she still felt exhausted. She shrugged in answer to Rory's question.

"Is there someone I can call? Do you need to go to the hospital?" Rory asked, pressing her for information.

Maura shook her head. There was no one to call. Her family was ill with the phocine virus, too. So many were scattered along the coast or dead. Tears welled in her eyes at the thought.

He continued asking her questions about how she was feeling. Was she hot? Was she cold? Maura was quiet and answered with a nod, shrug, or shake her head.

Finally, he asked, "Are you hungry?"

To this, she nodded and replied, "Yes."

"Okay," he said, "I'll be back in a few minutes with food."

He seemed nervous, and she wondered why. She was nervous, too. She didn't know what to expect of this man. He seemed kind, but, she thought, you never knew. She looked around the room again. There was another small room attached to this one. It had shiny tile. She put a foot out and then the other and stood up to investigate. She swayed when she stood. She was as weak as a newborn pup. Dizziness assailed her, and she had to sit. She rested her head against her knees until the feeling passed.

When the man returned, he saw her slumped over and cried out, "Oh no! Are you all right?"

He tugged, pulled a blanket around her, and handed her a plate with something warm, yellow, soft, and mushy piled on it, along with a piece of toasted bread spread with something that glistened.

The man looked sheepish and admitted, "I'm not much of a cook, but I can make scrambled eggs and toast."

Maura tried the food tentatively and found she liked the creamy taste of the eggs and the crunchy toast spread with a salty, creamy substance. She ate a few mouthfuls. This food was strange, and she marveled at the different textures. The toast was dry, and it made her cough. Rory gave her a fresh glass of water that he had brought in on the tray of food.

"Thank you," she said when the coughing ceased.

"It's not a problem," he assured her. After a moment, he added, "I'm Rory. Rory Sullivan."

Maura put a hand to her chest and said, "I'm Maura. Maura Muir."

"Hmm, alliterative," he returned with a smile.

She looked at him blankly.

The blanket slipped, revealing her breasts. Maura wasn't self-conscious, but Rory seemed embarrassed.

"I'll just go and find you something to wear," he said, practically running out of the room.

Maura looked at Rory's retreating form, and then she was distracted by the dog, sniffing hopefully but not eating the eggs on the plate.

"Go ahead," she told the dog. "I'm finished."

She stood again and went to the adjacent room. It was tiled in pale shades of chalky blues and grays like the sky. A long, low rectangular tub was in front of a window that framed the vista of the ocean. She fiddled with the knobs and was amazed when the water poured from the spigots. She played with the water, finding she could make it warm or cold. She decided to fill the tub like a warm, little tidepool. She couldn't resist and climbed in.

This water was so different from the ocean. It was clear and fresh. Maura loved it. She sank beneath the surface and peered up at the ceiling while she held her breath. A minute later, Rory's worried eyes looked at her. She emerged, looking at him with shining eyes and a small, shy smile.

"Ahh, you found the bathroom. Here's soap, and I'll put the towel and clothes over here," he told her, nodding to a small bench nearby.

The soap he handed her smelled sweet and lovely, like the flowers that grew along the edge of the sea. She rubbed the soap on her skin, relishing its silky smoothness.

"I'll leave you to it," Rory told her. He seemed embarrassed again. And he turned and left the room quickly.

Maura's eyes followed his retreating form. She shrugged. She wasn't embarrassed. What an odd man. She stayed in the little pool until the water cooled.

She felt weak again when she stood, and chills overcame her. She stood, dripping from the bath, goosebumps covering her. Rory returned to the bathroom.

"What's wrong?" he asked, looking at her worriedly.

Maura couldn't speak. She was freezing, and her teeth chattered. Rory came to the rescue and wrapped her in a towel.

"Let's get you dry and warm," he told her gently.

He helped her dry and put on sweatpants and a sweatshirt. Maura was unsure of the clothes. They seemed bulky yet much lighter than her pelt. They were soft in color and feel but not as soft as her fur. She patted at the pants and the shirt, hugging herself. He led her back to the bedroom, putting socks over her feet. These felt warm but constrictive. She wasn't sure about them.

"There, that should help," he said as he tucked her back into bed.

He also handed her a small blue pill and a glass of water, assuring her this would help alleviate her fever. Maura looked at the little blue pill and rolled it in her hand a moment before swallowing it. She lay back in the bed, balling herself up to keep warm. Maura moaned, and her teeth chattered. The dog moved closer to her, and it helped a little. Maura looked up at Rory, pleading in her eyes.

"S-s-s-so c-c-cold," she whispered.

4

RORY

Rory looked helplessly at Maura, shivering violently on the bed. He ran up the stairs to the linen closet and pulled out some blankets, bringing them down to pile them on top of Maura. Then he went to the kitchen to make her some hot, sweet tea. He helped her sit up and held the cup, telling her it was hot. It was difficult for her to sip as her teeth chattered, and she spilled tea on the blanket. She looked up at Rory helplessly. He sighed. There was only one way she was going to get warm, and that was with body heat.

"Move over, Skipper," he commanded the dog and snapped his fingers, pointing to the other side of the bed.

Skipper obeyed, grudgingly. He moved to Maura's side of the bed and flopped down, pinning her under the covers. Rory crawled into the bed beside her. He spooned with her, holding her tightly against him to warm her.

Their heartbeats were a polyphony, each one a separate melody, playing counterpoint and then harmonizing with each other in a few moments. Maura's shivers slowed to occasional shudders. She began to relax, and Rory did as well. It was only minutes until they both fell deeply asleep.

Hours later, Rory awoke to find his face buried in Maura's luxuriant black hair. It held the salty tang of the sea and fresh air. He breathed deeply, unperceptively moving closer as he did so. Her curves fit right into his as if they had been molded together in a previous time – puzzle pieces finally found and joined. He felt at utter peace and serenity holding Maura. And he realized, belatedly, that he was cupping her breast. No, make that clutching it. He released it, accidentally running a finger over a nipple that reacted immediately, becoming firm under his light touch. Maura made a sound Rory's body reacted.

He jumped out of the bed as if he had been burned. Guilt assailed him. She was ill. He didn't want to take advantage of her. He stared down at the sleeping Maura. Her cheeks were lightly flushed, and her beautiful, long, black hair was spread over the pillows. Her curves, under the sheets, were tantalizing. He wanted to run his hands over her petite frame and shapely curves. He wanted to breathe in her salty scent as he explored every inch of her body. Damn, his body! It was difficult to control the desire that flared within him. He wanted her in every way possible, and he stood, almost panting, above her. He found himself rubbing the bulge in his pants. He had to turn away.

5
MAURA

Wracked with cold, Maura was grateful when Rory came into the bed and held her. When his arm encircled her, and his body was pressed closely to hers, a sort of magic happened. It was a sensation of lightness, like clouds reflected on a peaceful sea. Maura felt a thrumming electric sensation in their bodies when they touched. What was happening to her? She did not expect to experience these sensations with a human. She should hate him, not be attracted to him. Her body betrayed her as it shifted to be closer to Rory. She was awed and comforted by his touch. His warm breath on the back of her neck calmed her with its steady rhythm. She finally fell asleep.

Waking later, she was feeling much better. The fever had abated, and she felt strangely relaxed but energized at the same time. It was as if his energy had cleansed her. Maura turned over to face Rory, and he looked at her in wonder with those eyes like pieces of the sea and sky. In his arms, she felt as safe as a scallop in its shell. She wasn't tired. She was contented. Supremely contented. Her mind drifted. Maura thought about how drastically her life changed in the last few weeks in a dreamy haze. Three to four weeks ago, seals from many herds started to get sick just as the weather turned colder. They had just started their trek south when the virus struck. Sick and dying seals were in every herd. Maura lost her mother. Her heart ached at the memory of the terror she saw in her mother's eyes as she labored for breath. Her sister, Rhona, became delirious from fever and disappeared. Maura didn't know if she was alive or dead. Her other sister, Kelsi, had left the herd long before the virus hit, escaping the unwanted attentions of the bully, Breach. He wanted to mate with Kelsi, and she wanted nothing of it. She went south months ago. Maura heard through the herd network that Kelsi had returned. Apparently, she swam north to share the news that she lived at a place that healed sick seals. Maura was on her way to visit Kelsi to tell her what had happened with their family. She missed her sisters, especially Kelsi. But the virus struck her, too. The last few days had been agony as she became gravely ill. She had struggled to breathe and swimming was difficult. She made little headway toward the place where Kelsi lived. One of the seals said it was somewhere south of Paumanok in New Jersey. It was past the great city that seemed to be a hive of millions of humans. It was a place she and other seals avoided. But, when she came ashore several hours ago, she thought it was the end of her life, too.

Rory and Skipper saved her. A tear leaked from her eye and slid down her cheek. Skipper raised his head, looked into her eyes, and thumped his tail.

Here she was, in human form and a human's bed. She could scarcely believe it. This was everything her grandmother, mother, and aunts warned her about. They told her humans would keep her pelt and make her a prisoner. Without her pelt, she was forced to remain a human. Maura crept out of bed to look for her pelt. It wasn't in the room where she was sleeping. She poked about cupboards and closets in the next few rooms. No pelt. What had Rory done with it? She looked at him again. Was he like the humans her family warned her about? She couldn't imagine Rory would keep her prisoner, but she didn't really know him. She suspected people were like some fish, hiding something fierce beneath a camouflage, like an octopus or a stonefish. Was Rory that way? And, if he was hiding her pelt to keep her prisoner, why had her instincts betrayed her? And her body? She had never felt an attraction to a seal or human in the past like this. This man stirred up a whirlpool of emotions and desires. Maura shivered, not only from the cold seeping through her but also from the questions niggling at her. She didn't want to believe her doubts about Rory. She wanted to crawl into the bed next to him and be held again, feeling safe and content.

Maura scooted into the space between Rory and Skipper, cocooning herself like seals on a beach. Skipper was another surprise. Here she was, liking a dog. She reached to scratch his ears.

Rory sighed in his sleep as she moved against him. Were Rory and Skipper her new family? Would she ever see Kelsi?

"Oh, Sedna," she whispered, pleading to the goddess, "Oh, Sedna, please help me."

6

RORY

Skipper pawed gently at Rory's shoulder until he awoke. He carefully extricated himself from the sleeping Maura and the bed.

"It's all right, boy," he told the dog. "I know you need to go out. You're probably hungry, too. Let's get you outside first."

Rory let Skipper run down to the beach. He watched him from the top of the stairs. Rory didn't know what time it was but thought it was nearing late afternoon when his stomach growled. He rubbed it absently. His mind was thinking about the beautiful woman sleeping inside.

But something about Maura filled his senses. His desire for her eclipsed his feelings for any other woman he had ever been with. It shocked him because they had just met. He wondered why. Skipper came bounding up the steps, dancing at his feet, tongue lolling. He looked expectantly at Rory, tail wagging.

"I know, boy. It's time for some grub. I must think of something for Maura and me to eat."

Skipper followed Rory inside, sat patiently, and wagged his tail as Rory prepared his kibble. He looked at Rory expectantly and with soulful eyes.

"Okay, boy. You've been amazing." He topped the kibble with some treats. Rory placed the bowl on the floor and stepped back. Skipper's head turned to follow Rory.

"Okay, go ahead, good boy," Rory told his dog absently as he went to the refrigerator to peer inside.

He heard a sound and turned. There was Maura, standing in the door-way, looking sexy with tousled hair, wearing only his sweatshirt that skimmed her bare bottom. He felt himself twitch and begin to swell. Rory took a deep breath, calming his desire.

"Hey," he said softly, "are you hungry?"

She glanced out the window and then nodded shyly.

"As I said before, I'm not a very great cook. I dabble, I guess. You?" he asked.

"N-no. I don't know how to cook," she answered. She glanced out at the ocean again.

"Well then, let me see what I have," he said, turning to look back inside the refrigerator.

"How does a tuna melt sound?"

"Lovely," Maura answered. "I love tuna."

Rory prepared the sandwiches and put them in a panini maker to heat them and melt the cheese. While they were cooking, he pulled out plates and potato chips.

The panini maker's timer dinged, and Rory put the steaming, savory sandwiches on the plates and took them to the table. He sat and motioned for Maura to join him. She sat across from him.

"Careful, the sandwiches might be hot," he cautioned her.

"Tuna melt?" she asked.

Rory picked up the sandwich and blew on it. He had taken a bite when she asked the question. It took him a moment to answer, "Yeah, tuna melt. You haven't had one before?"

"Well, I love tuna." Maura shrugged. "I just haven't eaten it like this."

"Oh?" Rory asked and added, "This is pretty good. It's tuna, mayo, capers, dill relish, and several good grinds of black pepper for the tuna salad. And the cheese, for melting, of course."

Rory wondered about her reaction to a simple tuna melt. It was as if she had never seen a sandwich before. Odd. Who didn't know about tuna sandwiches? The brief thought that she was lying skittered through his brain.

Maura nodded, quizzically looking at Rory and then at the sandwich.

She picked it up and took a bite. "It's good!" she said with delight and a tone of surprise.

"How do you like to eat tuna?" Rory asked.

"Umm, usually raw," Maura admitted.

"I like it that way, too. You must like sushi."

"Sushi?" Maura asked with wonder.

"You don't know what sushi is?" he asked, puzzled.

Maura shook her head.

"Where have you been?" he asked again, wondering about her honesty. He looked quickly around. Was this some kind of joke or comedic reality television program? There weren't any cameras, to his knowledge, as he had seen her naked.

"In New Brunswick, by the sea," she answered.

"Rural, huh?"

Maura nodded.

"How did you get here?"

"I swam," Maura told him simply.

Rory nearly choked on his sandwich. "What?" he asked, disbelieving.

"Yes, until I got sick," Maura admitted.

"I – I don't understand."

This woman was a complete puzzle. His mind drifted back to when he saw her on the beach. Was she crazy? How could she swim from New Brunswick to Long Island? It didn't make sense. He looked at his sandwich. He looked at Maura, wondering if he should believe what she was telling him.

"No, I don't suppose you would," Maura said, looking at him, interrupting his jumble of thoughts. Maura looked down at the remains of her sandwich.

He waited. She looked as though she wanted to ask him something, but the something was uncomfortable to ask. She shifted in the chair and fiddled with the sandwich. What was it? Would the truth be told now? He looked at Maura, silently asking her to continue.

Finally, she blurted out, "But, do you have my pelt?"

"Your pelt?" he asked, somewhat perplexed.

"Yes," Maura answered, "My sealskin. I am a Selki. Did you see my pelt?"

Rory stared at her, bewildered by her confession.

"I don't understand," he said, mystified.

7

MAURA

What was it with this guy? Maura thought. He didn't seem to have a clue. Maura looked at the remains of the sandwich on her plate. The human food was delicious and decidedly easier to obtain than chasing a tuna through the water. But the tuna wasn't important. She had to explain what a Selki was and ask about her pelt.

Maura cleared her throat and glanced at Skipper, who had curled under the table. She looked next at Rory. He looked expectantly at her.

"A Selki," she explained, "is a seal in the water and a human on land. I am a Selki," she ended with emphasis.

Rory stared at her. He stared. "A Selki?" he asked again.

"Yes, a Selki," she insisted.

"So...the cosplay, it's real?"

"I don't know what cosplay is," Maura admitted. "But my sealskin is part of me." Maura didn't admit to Rory that she couldn't return to the sea without her sealskin.

Rory rubbed his nose between his eyes, knocking his glasses a little askew. "Just so that I understand. What you're telling me is that you're a seal? And you're a human?"

Maura nodded. She could see the disbelief in his eyes.

"So...you're like Samantha in *Bewitched,* or maybe like Ruth in *Ancient Magus Bride?*" Rory asked.

Maura looked at him blankly. "I don't know what you're talking about."

Exasperated, Rory shook his head, almost in anger and definitely in disbelief. "I guess you wouldn't, being a seal," he said acerbically. "I'm just trying to wrap my head around the concept."

And, he added skeptically, "You speak English very well. You have a Canadian accent with a twist. If you're a Selki, how is that possible?"

Maura tried to keep her frustration and anger under control. He thought she was lying. She could tell by the tone of his voice and the shake of his head. Her eyes narrowed. Never had her integrity and honesty been in question. How dare he?

She was anxious to learn about her pelt, but she answered the question, "Seal and Gaelic are my first languages. My grandmother and aunts have had interactions with humans. They learned English and taught it to my mother and my sisters."

Rory stared at her and was mute. She continued that if he were a fish, he would need to get to the surface for air. He needed to know her story.

"That is, I can speak English, but I can't read or write," Maura admitted. Then, though through not quite gritted teeth, she asked, "And, my pelt? Do you have it?"

Rory looked up at her. He seemed surprised at first by the question and her tone before he answered, "Yeah, I mean, yes. It's in my shed, outside."

Maura relaxed and heaved a visible sigh of relief.

"So, it's safe?"

"Yes, yes, it's safe," Rory insisted.

"Thank Sedna!" Maura breathed.

"Thank, who?" Rory asked.

Maura looked at Rory, somewhat surprised. "Sedna," she answered, "the mother of us all."

This human was unbelievable. His skepticism bothered Maura. She would show him she was a Selki. That was the only way to win his belief in her. And she wondered for a moment if he was as trepidatious as she was about her presence here.

At that moment, the thought of getting back to the freedom of the sea was her foremost thought. Maura felt penned in by Rory's words. She knew he needed answers and was doing her best to answer his questions, but they were uncomfortable. Not having someone believe in her bothered her deeply. Seals didn't question one another. Their instincts were usually on target with truth.

"If we can get my pelt, I can show you I'm a Selki."

"Okay," Rory replied hesitantly.

Maura stood eagerly while Rory went to get his coat. Skipper waited by the door.

"Don't you want to put something on? The sweatpants are probably in the bedroom. I can get you a coat."

Maura shook her head. "I'll be putting on my pelt. And then, you'll see."

Rory shrugged and opened the door. Skipper practically danced outside, eager for them to join him on his walk.

Maura followed Rory to the shed. Twilight was gathering, and clouds scudded across the sky. The sea breeze tugged at her hair, whipping strands wildly about her body. She shivered a little, wishing she had put on the pants she had on earlier like he suggested. She watched as Rory unlocked the door to the small building and went inside. He returned with her pelt over his arm. Her pelt. She was so happy to have it back. She practically snatched it from him. She hugged it to her, holding it tightly, and then stroked it gently because for Maura, her pelt was like another limb. It was an intrinsic part of her.

Maura gestured towards the stairs, and Rory followed her. She went down the stairs, and the tide was very high. The incoming breakers spread almost to the stairs. Rory stood, watching her skeptically from the midpoint of the steps.

Maura took off the sweatshirt and carefully folded it. She stepped into her pelt, and immediately, it molded itself around her body. She pulled the hood-like head over her face and thrust her hands into the front flippers. She collapsed onto the sand, quickly pushed herself up by the flippers, and turned her head towards Rory. He looked astonished. She gave him a seal grin and scooched towards the water.

The waves broke around Maura, and she headed towards deeper waters. As soon as she could, she dove towards deeper water, greeting dolphins and stingrays as she swam. Maura twirled in the water, happy to be feeling better, enjoying the freedom of swimming in the open sea.

Her joy diminished, however, as her chest ached again, and her pelt felt as though it was weighing her down. Once again, she struggled to reach the surface. The illness. She couldn't stay in the sea and survive when she felt like this. She had to be in a safe place to heal. When she reached the surface, she saw Rory standing on the shore, gaping as he stared at the water.

There was something about this man that tugged at her heart, her brain, and her very soul. She didn't understand this. She just knew that she wanted to be near him – that she had to be near him. His worried gaze was like a siren's song, and she began to swim towards him.

Skipper could sense that she was coming. His paws danced in the sand. Rory glanced down at the dog and then back towards the sea. She swam as quickly as she could, panting a bit in her efforts to get to Rory quickly. The surf dumped her near the bottom of the stairs, and she looked up to Rory, standing mid-way before lowering her head and pawing back the hood to reveal her head, hair, and face. She removed her pelt, stripping out of it and putting it over her arm. Skipper, dancing in place on the dune grasses, raced toward her, butting her with his nose and licking her hand. She laughed and petted the dog before looking at Rory a little self-consciously. He looked at her, and she felt his gaze probe her heart and her brain. She almost felt helpless under his gaze, her body wanting to respond to him in a way she had never felt before. His gaze, even worried, reached deep inside and tugged at strings of joy within her. These human emotions awed Maura. She returned his gaze with wonder.

She climbed the stairs and stopped before him, Skipper pressing his body into her pelt and legs.

"A Selki," he murmured, astonished.

Maura gave a small laugh. "Yes, a Selki," she replied, following him up the stairs back into the house, a small, satisfied smile on her lips, knowing now he believed her.

8

RORY

ory gaped as Maura stepped into the sealskin, which almost seemed to swallow her as it molded to her body. She changed into a seal. How could this happen? He rubbed his eyes and blinked, doubting what he was seeing. He looked again, and the seal turned its head toward him, joy evident. He watched her as she moved toward the ocean, nosed into the water, and disappeared into the waves.

Twilight was gathering, and it was difficult to see the bobbing seal head. It would appear, glance at him, and vanish again beneath the water. She swam far out, and he wondered what was living out in the deeper ocean. He would have to ask her, that is if she came back.

He believed her now – that she was a Selki. But, as many fantasy and science fiction books he had read or films he had seen, it didn't prepare him for the reality of Maura transforming into a seal. He stared at the ocean, hoping to catch a glimpse of her.

Would she come back? And did he want her to return? In his heart, he knew he did. There was something about Maura that he felt a connection to that he wasn't sure he had experienced before. It was something almost corny, like saying it was 'magic.' And how was that even possible?

Rory glanced at Skipper, who waited patiently on the dune grass. He seemed expectant, too, as if he knew she would return.

Would she? And, if she did, what then? He watched the bobbing seal head move further into the open ocean until it was only a speck on the water. Was the seal head real, or his imagination, he wondered as he squinted at the water, trying to see better. He wasn't sure at this point. He had an unexpected ache in his heart and felt bereft. No, he felt emptier than he had ever felt in his life.

Skipper gave a bark and then a whine. It was his sound when he was worried. Rory called to him, but his usually obedient dog didn't move. It was as if he was glued to the sand. He continued to whine and stare out at the ocean.

Rory called Skipper again. The dog didn't budge. Rory looked out at the ocean where Skipper was staring. Was that a seal head? Was it coming closer? Was it Maura? The closer the head moved in the water towards the shore, the more excited Skipper became. He wagged his tail, sending sand flying, and his paws danced as he stayed in his spot.

Finally, he saw the seal's head and then the body. The breakers seemingly dumped the seal at the bottom of the steps to his house. The flippers pawed at the head and Maura's beautiful face and luxuriant hair emerged from beneath the seal head that now looked like a hood. She peeled the sealskin from her body like a tight, wet bathing suit and stood, beautiful and glorious in the falling night.

Skipper was beside himself. He raced to Maura when she emerged and butted her with his nose, and licked her with his happy, doggy noises.

Maura looked up at Rory. He thought her glance was a little shy.

When she reached him, all he could murmur was, "A Selki, eh?"

She smiled, and her smile lit up her face, "Yes."

But then Maura doubled over coughing. The swim must have been too much for her. Rory put his arm around her, supporting her.

"Here, let me take the sealskin. We'll take it into the house, okay? It will be with you," he assured her.

Maura couldn't answer. The coughing overtook her. Rory led her back to the bedroom, tucked her in the bed, and placed the sealskin beside her on the floor. He raced to the kitchen to get a glass of water. Inspired, he reached into the cupboard for the whiskey bottle. Hadn't his grandmother made cough syrup from equal parts of honey, whiskey, and lemon? He heard Maura's wracking cough and didn't have time to make cough syrup. He poured a dram of whiskey into a small glass and took whiskey and water into Maura.

He helped her by holding the glass as she sipped the water between coughs. Her fever had returned, but it wasn't as rampant. Her forehead was warm, not as hot as before. He gave her another pill along with the sips of water and urged her to drink the whiskey. She looked surprised and grimaced at the taste. Rory wanted to laugh, but he was relieved it seemed to settle the cough. She lay back down and closed her eyes. Rory pulled the covers up around her. Skipper snuggled in beside her.

He suspected the exertion of the swim, combined with her illness, was wearing Maura out. With the cough settled, he smoothed the blankets around Maura and his dog as best he could. Glued to Maura, Skipper looked up at him with soulful eyes and slowly thumped his tail.

"Good boy," Rory whispered. "You take care of her."

A Selki? It was difficult to wrap his head around the reality of a Selki existing. What had only been fantasy he read or viewed in movies was happening in his life. He felt shaky and had to lean against the counter. It was so surreal. Again, his brain drifted to the thought of hidden cameras and that this was some sort of strange joke. If so, why and why him? And, if Selkis were real, what else was real? It rocked his perception of the world. And, she returned to him rather than head back out to sea. Why? Because she was ill? Or was it the connection he felt with Maura earlier? He wondered if she felt it, too. He had never given thought to the 'love at first sight' crap. Or, at least, that's what he always thought it was – crap. But he experienced something in Maura's presence, almost like an invisible joining. And it was astonishing.

Now what? The weekend was over, and he needed to get back to work tomorrow. He was grateful he worked from home, but it still posed several problems. Maura needed clothes, and they needed groceries. He glanced at the time.

He returned to the guest bedroom. Maura was sleeping soundly. He told Skipper to take care of her and grabbed his keys. His mind whirled as he drove to the store, thinking all that he needed to purchase. Maura needed clothes, and underthings, and shoes, and the list went on and on. She didn't seem to have a clue about the human world from what he observed thus far.

He pulled into the parking lot. Food was easiest, he thought. She seemed to like the scrambled eggs and the tuna. He could pick up a variety of fish, chowders, and more eggs. He filled his cart with fresh, frozen, canned seafood delights and staples before heading to the womenswear section.

Rory was overwhelmed by the variety of clothing and lingerie. Maura was small, but he couldn't remember the word for women of smaller stature. She was also zaftig – not fat, just curvy. Her beautiful breasts were lusciously plump, like juicy grapefruits. He felt his jeans grow tight again, thinking about her.

Rory wished he could call his mom. She always said she could and would talk with him about anything, but he didn't think a shape-changing seal woman would be in the mix of topics. Mom was tall, lean, and Scandinavian-looking with her blond hair aging to a brilliant white, startlingly blue eyes, and fair skin. She was anything but petite. That was the word, petite. Maura was petite. He looked at the clothing, overwhelmed by the choices, and seeing things his mother and grandmother wouldn't be caught dead in. He reached into his pocket for his phone, about to dial his mom, imagining their conversation, "Uh, mom? I need to buy clothes for a Selki. Yeah, she is a seal, but she's a woman. She's petite..." That wouldn't work. He put his phone away, sighing. He leafed through the racks. He was so confused. There weren't any clerks in sight at this box store. There were a few people wandering around. There was an older woman, maybe his mom's age. She looked nice.

"Excuse me," he said, blushing a little. "Can you help me? I'm looking for stuff for a friend that's sick. Um, I don't know what size she is."

The older woman with graying hair leaned on her shopping cart and looked at him quizzically. "A friend you say?" She gave him the hairy eyeball that questioned his motives.

"It's a new friend," he stammered. "She – she lost her luggage coming from Canada and now has the flu. I need to get her some clothes." He hoped he wouldn't trip up in his lie.

"How tall is she? Is she large or small?" the woman asked, her voice gravelly, and she sounded like she could mean business

Rory raised his hand to his chest, "She's petite and," he blushed again, feeling like he was thirteen, "she's," he fought to find a word and finally settled on, "curvy." He moved his hands in a way to mimic Maura's size. He could tell the woman was holding back a smile after his gestures.

"You probably need petite clothes. This isn't the best store for that.

Maybe leggings that stretch and tunic sweaters would work," the woman advised.

She pulled a few things off the racks.

"Here, these might do," she told him, stretching a pair of leggings in front of his eyes. "And, over there," she pointed to a rack, "some sweaters aren't too bad."

"Thanks," he said. "You've been very kind."

"Good luck," she commented before she exited with a wink. Lingerie was another nightmare. He guessed again, choosing athletic bras and some panties because the couple of women who came through the lingerie department avoided him and wouldn't meet his eyes. He felt extremely conspicuous going through the bits of lace and satin. The jumble of clothing made a colorful mound in his cart. He was overwhelmed and knew it. The smell of the new clothing was giving him a headache. He thought this was enough for a start and headed to check out.

9

MAURA

$\mathcal{M}$aura woke feeling much better. The fever was gone and she felt more alive than in weeks. She lay in the bed, listening. The house felt empty of Rory's presence., but she wasn't sure. Skipper was pressed into her and he opened an eye as she shifted and yawned. She patted his head.

Where was Rory? She got out of bed and Skipper stretched and moved into the warm spot she left. He closed his eyes.

Maura padded to the kitchen and looked around. No Rory. She hadn't been beyond the bedroom, bathroom, or kitchen. She walked into the next room. It was spacious, with a table and chairs near the entrance to the kitchen. Stairs stretched up to another floor. She walked past the table and chairs to the windows that stretched from floor to ceiling and was mesmerized by the sight of the sea. It was stunning to see the smoky blue water in the falling light. Shadows gathered, and the sky was a deep, deep blue. It was the color just between twilight and nightfall. Maura pulled herself away. She would come back, sit, and look in a minute, but first, she needed to see if Rory was truly gone. And where was he? He wouldn't go to the beach without Skipper. She looked around the room. A large couch and a few chairs were placed to look out the magnificent windows. On the other side of the room was a smaller couch and grouping of chairs that looked out over the yard and were grouped near a black iron box set on bricks. It had a pipe that led up to the roof.

She walked around, feeling the textures of the upholstery. The couch was soft, almost like a pelt. The chair had a nubby feel and had a lot of texture, like a bumpy shell, only softer The black iron box was cold to the touch. She looked about. There were books of all sizes on the shelves. On the table, there were photographs of Rory with different people. One was a tall, white-haired woman. They had the same eyes. She wondered if it was his mother. More photographs with Rory and people his age. One was a woman who was as tall as he and stocky. They were laughing and were wearing large hats. It was a silly picture. Another photograph was with some guys with Rory. They had their arms draped around each other and were all wearing dress-like tunics and square hats with tassels. Rory looked happy in all the photographs. Without thinking, Maura traced over his face lightly with one finger. Next, she looked at the paintings. There was a large painting depicting the lighthouse at the end of Paumanok. She had hauled out there a few times on the beach south of the lighthouse. She remembered looking at the lighthouse and wondering what it would be like to live within four walls. There was another painting of a calm sea, its color nearly matching the sky with the sun setting. The waves sparkled with a path of golden light and the ribbons of a colorful sunset tinged the clouds She liked the calm colors of the room in varied hues of blues and grays. It was peaceful. The floor was tile that looked like wood. It was cool to walk on in her bare feet, like hard packed sand. She liked it and went up the stairs.

Here, she found more rooms. One was obviously Rory's bedroom. It, too, looked out over the sea. It was peaceful and very masculine, decorated with gray walls and deep browns. Maura looked at the bed and went over and touched it. It smelled of Rory. When she put her hand on the bed, she felt vestiges of his energy left in the bedclothes. Her abdomen fluttered. It was all she could do not to throw herself on the bed and absorb the energy left there. She wanted to roll around in his bedclothes, smell his smell, and feel his presence. She resisted, moving further into the room and peeking into another bathroom. This one was also tiled in blues and grays like the one downstairs.

Down a short hallway was another room. Books lined a wall, and a desk with electronics faced the ocean. Like everywhere else in the house, things were spare and neat. A large drafting table was ensconced behind the desk. Maura looked at the drawings lying there. It looked like a house, and boxes representing rooms were also drawn. They were labeled, but Maura couldn't read. The letters looked like strange marks to her.

There was another room upstairs at the very end of the hall. It was smaller than the others and was virtually empty except for a couch and a desk. Its creamy, buttery walls held the light that poured in from the large windows. Maura liked it, thinking the smaller space was cozy.

She returned to the living room, sat on the couch, and gazed at the ocean. It was so odd for her to see the ocean from this perspective. She was always in the ocean, looking towards the shore. She had seen the beach and houses in many of her travels up and down the coast.

Gazing at the ocean, she could almost feel the currents, the waves, and the pull of the tide. She could feel the energy of the water and all the creatures within. They called to her. The pull was strong. Part of her wanted to be out in that expanse of ocean, looking back at the beach and the houses. But the night was falling. Night on the ocean was treacherous. Sharks were sneaky, grabbing a seal in the deep shadows of darkness and tearing it to shreds. She shuddered. Sharks were terrifying. Their dead eyes held nothing except the knowledge that they wanted to eat you. Maura had narrowly escaped from being caught by a shark. Dolphins saved her, butting the shark with their hard noses to distract it so that she could make an escape. She was eternally grateful to them.

A sound woke her from her reverie. Maura heard Skipper jump off the bed, claws clattering across the floor as he ran into the kitchen. Startled, Maura turned and saw Rory in the doorway, his head surrounded by the aura of light from the kitchen. It wasn't as bright as when she first glanced up at him from the beach and the sun was a halo behind him, but the light of the kitchen mirrored his aura. She nearly gasped at her untoward reaction to him. There it was. He had returned, and the empty hollow in her body was filled again. The happiness it caused astonished her. She couldn't tear her gaze from him. She barely heard him say, 'hello.' Maura stood and automatically moved towards Rory, feeling a need to get physically closer to him. In the ocean, a buzz and an undercurrent of electric-like sensation connected all the living things within the sea. It was like that with Rory. She felt a buzz of energy that connected them, and the closer she got to him, the more it grew. It was exciting but also comforting. It was as if that energy pulled them together and created a pool of serenity.

10

RORY

*R*ory grabbed the bags from the store and entered the house quietly, thinking Maura might still be asleep. Skipper raced from the bedroom, tongue lolling. Rory put the bags on the floor and reached out one hand to pet him. He walked quietly to the bedroom doorway and peered in. No Maura. Puzzled, he went to the entrance to the great room, where he saw Maura sitting, staring at the ocean.

She was sitting, nestled in a corner of the couch, her knees drawn up. Her long, dark hair was a soft puddle draping along the back of the couch and down her body. She turned those lovely, large, dark pools of eyes to look at him. When her eyes focused on him, pulling her from her daydream, she smiled involuntarily at the sight of him. His insides grew warm as he took in her expression.

"Hey there," he said softly, taking her in like a long draught of cold, clear water on a hot day. Seeing her was a need. And now, with Maura in front of him, he felt astonishingly whole again.

Maura stood up from the couch and came over to him. Part of him wanted to grab her and pull her to him. It had only been a little more than an hour since he had been gone. It surprised him that it felt like he had been away for hours.

"I've been to the store," he told her. "And I picked up a few things. Come and see." He motioned for her to come into the kitchen. She followed. Rory showed her the purchases, and she seemed rather nonplussed by the clothes, fingering the textures. She seemed particularly taken by the softness of the nightgown.

"Put it on," he urged Maura. "Go ahead."

Without embarrassment or guile, Maura took off the sweatshirt she was wearing. She stood unembarrassed at her nudity. Rory felt himself twitch and begin to grow hard again. What was happening to him? Her very presence sent his desire into orbit. He had to look away and nervously tore at the tag to remove it from the nightgown before giving it to Maura to put on. It wasn't a sexy clothing item, but the soft cotton hugged her curves. The only thing Rory wanted to do was to run his hands up and down her body, feeling the curves beneath the cotton knit before removing it and seeing her glorious naked body beneath it again. He gulped, tamping down his desire.

"Hungry?" he almost spluttered.

Maura nodded. Rory busied himself, removing groceries from bags and showing them to her. She seemed fascinated by the pictures on the cans and boxes. She seemed particularly taken by the fisherman at the wheel of a boat on the box of frozen fish.

He interrupted her reverie, holding up a can. "I was thinking about some salmon chowder?"

She nodded. Maura followed him like Skipper as he put the groceries away. He showed her the small pantry, with shelves partially filled with canned and boxed food.

"What is all this?" Maura asked.

Rory wrinkled his forehead, thinking how to explain. Realization hit him that she likely had never seen canned or processed foods.

"It's called a pantry. These are some of the things I eat," he explained. "I go to a store and the food is already prepared so that I can cook and eat it. I store extra food here so it's easy to prepare when hungry."

Maura's mouth formed a small "O" before she said, "That's amazing. That makes it so easy to get food. Seals are constantly looking for their next meal."

He closed the door to the pantry and opened the freezer. Maura's eyes widened as the cold air whooshed out. She held up her hands, surprised at the change in temperature. He liked the look of wonder in her eyes. It was endearing. The freezer, another new experience.

"It's called a freezer," he explained. "To keep the food frozen and fresh until I'm ready to use it."

He nearly laughed at the expression on her face as she peered at the frozen food and held her hands to the cold air. Next, he pulled out a pan and the can opener. Maura was fascinated when he opened the can, and she saw the soup inside. Knowing she had likely never seen someone cooking on a stove, he modeled the process of heating the soup.

"You see, the food is in the can. I can pull out a pan, put the soup in it, and heat it on the stove. When it's warm, we can eat it. It tastes better that way, at least to humans. You have to be careful with the stove, and it can get very hot," he explained. "Here, hold out your hand, like you did with the freezer, but don't touch."

Maura did as told and moved closer to the warmth. Rory pointed out how the burner became red when it was hot but warned her it could still be hot to the touch. He turned off the burner for a minute and showed her the "HS" symbol on the stove's controls, which indicated a "hot surface." Maura nodded that she understood.

While it was heating, he moved to the cupboard to get bowls and spoons. He also pulled out a sleeve of crackers. These he placed on the table with a knife and a stick of butter. Once the soup was heated, he poured it into the bowls and put the empty saucepan into the sink, running a little water to fill it. He took the bowls of soup to the table and invited Maura to sit with him. Maura had been silent while she observed him cooking. She sniffed the salmon chowder appreciatively when she sat down. He showed her how to blow on the hot soup on his spoon to eat it, and she followed his example.

She made an appreciative sound at the first taste, and he smiled.

"It's good, isn't it?" he asked her.

"Very," she agreed.

Rory spread some butter on the saltines and made a small sandwich of the crackers. He handed one to her.

"I remember that you liked butter this morning. It's made from the milk of cows," he explained.

Maura tried the small cracker sandwich tentatively. He was amused by her surprise at the crumbliness of the crackers. She closed her eyes at the delicious taste of butter. He spread more butter on the crackers and laid out the little cracker sandwiches on the small plate he brought to the table.

He liked butter on crackers, too. There was something comforting about it, but he had a history. His grandmother gave him cracker sandwiches with soup his whole life. They reminded him of her and the comfort of being with his Besta. That's what he called his grandmother, from his mother's Scandinavian roots. His Besta always told him she was his 'bestest' friend, enjoying the play on words. He wondered what Besta would think of Maura. She was a big one for folklore and would have likely fallen in love with Maura and grilled her about a Selki's life. It was through Besta that he learned about folklore from around the world. She always believed in magic being in the world. She would frequently tell him to 'look for the magic. "It's all around us, Rory. It's really there. Knowing there is magic in this world will get you through many tough times. You just need to remember." He could hear his grandmother's voice. He lost himself for a few moments in the memory. He missed her. She was someone who would believe Maura was a Selki. Besta would have questioned Maura about Selki and Selki life, likely asking all the right questions.

He looked up to see Maura staring at him. Slightly embarrassed, he told her, "I was remembering my grandmother. She loved to make me these cracker sandwiches. It was a good memory."

Maura nodded, "I loved my grandmother too. She didn't make cracker sandwiches, but I danced with her in the sea and on the sand."

"Danced?" he questioned.

"Yes. Selkis' on the beach in the moonlight," she told him. "Usually under a full moon."

"Out of your sealskins?" he asked.

"Why, yes, of course!" Maura laughed, "How could we dance in our sealskins?"

Her look of complete astonishment surprised Rory.

"I don't know anything about Selkis," he admitted. "It's just a story or two I read as a boy and, I think, a movie I once saw. It's as new to me as the human world is to you."

She softened immediately and explained, "On nights of the full moon, we leave the ocean, shed our skins, and dance and celebrate under the moon. My sister, Kelsi, is very musical and sings beautifully. She's constantly making up songs and mimicking the music of the wind and the sea, but putting it to a melody."

Maura closed her eyes and swayed a little. Rory imagined several naked Selkis dancing in the moonlight. One of them was Maura, sitting across from him. His desire for her twitched in his pants. He cleared his throat.

"It must be beautiful, dancing in the moonlight."

"Oh, it is!" Maura replied passionately. "There's nothing like it. You should try it sometime."

Rory laughed. "Maybe I will. Do you sing?"

Maura hesitated before answering, "I do. I'm not half as good as Kelsi, but I like to sing. I love to dance. And I love to make patterns of rocks, shells, and seaweed on the sand." Looking down and slightly embarrassed, she stated, "I call them sand paintings. It takes hours to put them together, and they're like an offering to Sedna and the sea. The sea takes them away as the tide rises," she finished rather mournfully.

"I think I would like to see your sand painting sometime," Rory commented.

"Really?" Maura asked.

Her eyes were huge in surprise at his request. They were deep pools of liquid brown, almost black. There was an innocence in her expression. Maura was truly discovering interaction with humans. Rory mulled over this thought. He wanted to introduce her to many different things and see the wonderment in her eyes.

"Really," he insisted. "Or, maybe you could draw it for me."

"Draw?" Maura asked.

"Come with me," he stood, placing their bowls in the sink.

Rory left the kitchen, motioning for Maura to follow him upstairs to the room with the drafting table. He took paper from a machine and a thin object from a container on the desk.

"Drawing," he explained, "is one of the ways to make art in a two-dimensional form."

He quickly sketched Maura, capturing the details of her face in just a few strokes.

"Oh!" Maura cried. "Is that me?"

"Well, I'm not very good," Rory said. "I just dabble, but yes, it's a quick sketch of you."

Maura sucked in a breath. "It's lovely."

He handed it to her. "It's yours."

She took the drawing and held it to her as if it was precious, "Thank you."

Rory was a little embarrassed by her show of emotion over a simple drawing. He turned to grab another sheet of paper from the printer. He handed the pencil and paper to Maura. He took her hand, showing her how to hold the pencil.

"Now, you try," he said.

Maura stared at him, and he took her hand and the pencil and gently pressed them to the paper.

"See," he said, "the pencil marks the paper. You can create anything you want."

"Oh!" Maura cried as she saw their hands make marks on the paper.

He guided her hand, showing her how to make circles, ovals, and squares. When he let her hand go, she stood, bent over the paper, and began to make her designs. He opened a desk drawer and pulled out a pad of paper. He also had some graphite pencils. He turned to look at what she had drawn thus far.

Maura began drawing a complex mandala, and sketching the parts of stones, sticks, seaweed, and shells. Her rendition of the natural objects was like photo-realism in the rendering. The black and white strokes were meticulous creating a life-like scene on the paper. And this was her first time to draw? She was a natural-born artist with incredible talent. Now he was in awe. "Wow!" he breathed loud enough for Maura to hear.

She turned to him, showing him a brilliant smile.

"This is a drawing of one I created before. I love drawing!" she added exuberantly. "Why, I could draw all the time. I have so many mandalas in my head, but usually, they're determined and influenced by what I find on the shore," she stated, waving a hand at the paper and pencil. "I think I could spend hours and hours putting my images onto paper."

"Well, you can," Rory laughed. "The pencil you're using is just one medium. There are so many you can explore. But, you might like this more," Rory said, offering her the pad of drawing paper and graphite pencils. "You'll be able to do better shading with these pencils,"."

He was going to tell her about painting, but Skipper was at the door. He barked and danced.

"Okay, boy. I know you probably need to go out," Rory told the dog. Then he turned to Maura and asked, "Do you want to take a walk?"

He realized she was in a nightgown then and wore no shoes. Shoes! He had forgotten shoes.

Maura nodded, but Rory shook his head, "You can't go out like that. It's cold. And I forgot shoes at the store. I wonder what size feet you have?"

He looked down at her feet and realized she had extraordinarily long toes. Her feet were large in comparison to her body. He realized, belatedly, that this was probably because she was also a seal. They had flippers with long toes within. He put his foot next to Maura's. He didn't have an overly large foot. He wore a size ten shoe. Their foot sizes almost matched. He wondered what size ten was for a woman's shoe size. He would need to look it up.

Rory went to the closet and looked inside at the shoe rack. He reached inside and pulled out a pair of slip-on black stretchy mesh shoes.

"Here, these should work until we can get to a store."

He helped Maura into the shoes and then grabbed a hoodie for her to wear.

"I hope you'll be warm enough," he told her. "We'll only be out for a few minutes. Skipper doesn't like the dark and does his business at night fairly quickly."

Maura nodded at what he said but tentatively stepped around the bedroom in her shoes. She tried walking and followed Rory and Skipper carefully down the stairs and out the door. Skipper raced on ahead to the yard. He did not go down the stairs to the beach tonight.

It was a beautiful night. It was still warm for early December, but the breeze held the promise of winter. The stars sparkled in the dark sky. Once again, he was grateful his summer neighbors were not around, and he could see the constellations and even the swathe of the Milky Way in its full glory. He stretched his head back to gaze at the stars. He could see Ursa Major and Ursa Minor. The sky was extraordinarily clear. A falling star whizzed across the sky.

Involuntarily he said, "Make a wish."

"What?" Maura asked.

"Make a wish on the falling star," he instructed, pointing quickly to the meteor disappearing over the dark ocean.

"You do that too?" Maura asked, surprised at his direction.

"Yes," he said, "all my life. When I was small, my mom would have me say, "Star light, star bright, first star I see tonight. I wish I may; I wish I might have the wish I wish tonight." I also said it when I saw a falling star."

"We would wish on stars, too," Maura told him. "My grandmother said the gods would be peering down at us, and a star would come loose in the sky and fall."

He turned and looked at her. Her long hair wafted around her. Her large, dark eyes captured the starlight. He moved towards her, wanting to take her in his arms and kiss her, but Skipper raced between them, tongue lolling. He was ready to get back inside the house.

With the magic broken, Rory said, "Okay, Skipper. We're headed back inside. Come on."

11

MAURA

Maura could feel herself fading. She leaned on the kitchen island and yawned and yawned.

"You should get to bed," Rory advised. "You've been so ill."

She nodded, not protesting in the least. She removed the jacket he had loaned her and stepped out of the shoes before heading to the bedroom. Skipper followed her. She crawled into bed, pulling the covers around her. Without her pelt, she was cold. Skipper jumped up beside her, pressing against her. She was happy with his warmth but wished Rory was beside her.

There was a moment outside when she thought he would pull her to him. She wondered about kissing a human and what that would feel like. What would it feel like with Rory?

She drifted into thoughts of the day, including the sketching. Oh, Sedna, how she loved drawing! It brought what she imagined into visual life. She was itching to draw more and possibly get to the beach to make mandalas again. It was one of her favorite activities while ashore and out of her sealskin. Her mind whirled with the possibilities she could create by drawing and on the beach. With sketching, she could plan what she wanted to create on the shoreline. She might have to switch out some materials, but she would be able to recreate everything she had in her imagination. Designs danced in her head as she drifted into sleep.

Her subconscious worked in mysterious ways. Sometime later, her lovely dreams of mandala designs switched to a nightmare. Maura dreamed of swimming in the dark ocean with the stars shining all around. It was joyful to watch the heavens. The stars seemed to dance, and she gave a happy trill.

And then, a sleek, dark shape brushed against her. She froze for a moment. It wasn't another seal or a fish—it was a shark! Maura screamed and writhed, trying to swim as fast as she could, but she could sense the shark, and she screamed and screamed in seal language and human language. White-hot panic enveloped her.

Suddenly, Rory was there, patting her arm, talking to her, and asking if she was all right. He took her in his arms and held her tightly. Maura buried her face in his shirt, sobbing and crying, "Shark! Shark!"

He assured her there was no shark. He crooned and held her, and her sobs diminished slowly. It was then that he kissed her. He kissed her hair and nose and, finally, a tentative, soft kiss to her mouth. Maura was dazzled by the emotions released from that kiss. Her entire body reacted. It was like being deluged by a wave and then floating in its wake, every cell on her pelt awash with joy at being in the water. She closed her eyes and wanted to drink in the sensations. Her lips were on fire, and she wanted more. She kissed him back. And with that, he kissed her more hungrily, tasting her, his tongue darting in and around her mouth like a small fish. She discovered she liked it, wanting his kisses to envelop her. She wanted Rory to kiss her all over. The thought of his lips on her bare skin was tantalizing. She pressed against him. It was more than a wish now; it was a need.

His hand brushed her breast, and her nipple reacted. She moaned involuntarily. The feeling was so incredible that she looked at him in wonder. He pulled back then and looked at her questioningly.

He held a question. He kissed her again gently and asked, "Are you sure?"

Maura nodded mutely and permitted him to continue. That was all the invitation he needed. He released her from her clothing and then worked to rid himself of his, tossing everything on the floor beside him. Their bodies nestled in the bedclothes, Rory kissed Maura again, lightly, beginning at her hair and kissing her face and mouth gently. He trailed south, kissing her neck and traveling south to her breasts. Maura moaned.

She cried out in surprise and pleasure when he sucked on her nipples. They reacted to his kisses, becoming taut with her excitement. She squirmed on the bed, and Rory went further south in his kisses.

He spread her legs gently and fingered her. She was so wet. He entered her, ever so slowly and completely. She felt an initial sharp pain but then felt as though she had come home. They lay there a few moments, him fully inside of her for a moment, feeling their bodies joined as one.

Maura cried out, arching beneath him, wanting him to dive deeper as he moved within her, slowly and deliberately. This lovemaking was so very different from what seals did. Rory was so very tender and touched her so that she could have pleasure. Seal bodies didn't bend and move like this, and she felt her limbs grow liquid in their pleasure. She wanted to move beneath Rory so she could feel him inside as deeply as possible. He seemed to enjoy her movements. And then, he became more frantic, and she did as well. Their climax together brought cries of pleasure and passion ringing out in the room. Maura was stunned by it all. Especially when, afterwards, Rory gathered her in his arms like she was precious, his face pressed against her hair. He seemed to want to drink her in, and Maura was happy to comply. This mating with a human was nothing like what she saw in the seal world.

She had avoided mating with a seal, as did her sister. Kelsi had run away to the shores of New Jersey, and now she was with a human. Maura could now understand Kelsi wanting to mate with a human. She had never experienced the range of sensations and the joy from mating. And she wanted more. She wondered if Rory did. He seemed like he wanted to mate. He definitely enjoyed it. Maura did, too. She snuggled into his arms more deeply. She felt as safe as a scallop in a shell in his arms. Her body was lit from within, and she felt like she was glowing like the stars outside and like the magic of a bioluminescent sea. Rory was asleep and breathing calmly and steadily. Their heartbeats seemed to move as one, and Maura's breathing fell into rhythm with Rory's. She slept. With Rory, the nightmares vanished.

12

RORY

The alarm on Rory's phone had been turned to vibrate. Its soft persistence staccato woke him. He turned it off and wrapped himself around Maura again. She had stirred but was sleeping so deeply she did not wake. He breathed in her scent, which had a hint of sweetness and saltiness.

Monday. It was time to return to reality. But his reality had changed drastically this weekend. His world had been shattered and reborn with the knowledge that Selkis existed. And Maura, she had blown his world apart. He understood the term 'head over heels in love' now. It was like he was under some spell with her and couldn't get enough of her. Their weekend had ended spectacularly with their lovemaking, and he wanted more. So much more.

He couldn't resist her bare breast and rosy nipple peeking out from beneath the comforter, begging to be touched, licked, and sucked. He rose up on one elbow and did just that. It became instantly erect, as did he. And then, he gently sucked on her nipple, breathing in as he did so, the cooling air making it more rigid. She moaned in pleasure and awakened slowly.

When her eyes flew open, he stopped his assault and wished her a good morning, his eyes twinkling mischievously. He could see her eyes were filled with desire for him to continue, and he heard her whisper, "Don't stop."

So, he didn't. Rory continued to twirl his tongue around her nipple. He fingered the other one. Maura began to squirm. He wanted to taste every inch of her and kissed and licked his way south until his mouth and tongue settled on her soft pearl. He loved tasting her slightly salty skin. It was addictive. When his tongue circled her clitoris, she bucked wildly and arched her back to get closer to his mouth. He continued and then lapped up her salty juices as if he couldn't get enough.

He stopped then and looked at her. Maura's deep, dark eyes shone with awe and passion. Rory grinned. He couldn't help it and entered her. This time, he wasn't as slow and gentle. He thrust into her deeply, and she moaned in pleasure, raising her hips to meet him. She felt so good, tightly wrapped around his length. Thrust after thrust brought him to new heights of sensation. Maura's rapturous cries of pleasure drove him on until they climaxed. They cried out as one in ecstasy.

"Wow," he breathed afterward. "You are incredible, Maura."

She looked embarrassed. "I don't see how. I had never mated before. I didn't know it could be pleasurable."

Rory started. "What?" he asked incredulously. "You were a virgin? You never...never..." his words trailed off. Guilt assuaged him, at first, replaced by a sense of pride that he didn't expect. Maura certainly responded to their lovemaking as passionately as he did.

"No," she admitted, "I never mated before with either a seal or a man."

"And, what do you think of it?" he asked, a naughty glint in his eye.

Shyly and a little coyly, she answered, "I like it very much. I want to mate with you again and again. I don't think I could ever get enough."

He laughed at this with a great belly laugh. What man wouldn't want to hear that from a woman? He was a lucky man, he thought. This was the stuff normally relegated to romance movies, not reality.

"What?" she asked, slightly offended.

He sobered, "I will do everything in my power to make that wish come true. But, right now, I need to get ready to work."

"Work?"

"Yes, I'm an architect—an independent one. I help create buildings and additions, or whatever is needed."

"I don't understand," Maura replied, looking confused.

Remember those drawings on my drafting table upstairs?"

Maura nodded.

"They're my drawings. I work on plans to build buildings. All those boxes and marks on the paper represent buildings and the rooms inside. I'm in the middle of a project right now. I'm having difficulties with a contractor. Mind you, he's good, really, really good, but he's not very reliable, and I have a project deadline. I can't meet the deadline if he only works part-time or doesn't communicate with me," Rory completed with frustration. "I'll be on the phone and the computer a large part of the day. I may need to go to the building site. You'll be on your own a bit. Is that all right?"

"You're taking Skipper?" she asked.

"No! No, Skipper stays here," he said.

"Then, I won't be alone," Maura said. "He's a good hound."

"He is that," Rory chuckled again and suggested, "Let's get cleaned up and get some breakfast before I need to work. And I'm going to shower upstairs, and not with you. I can't get distracted anymore, even though I want to." He looked at her, desire glowing like embers in his eyes. And then he added, "I can help you with the human clothing. And I'll pick up shoes on my way home for you. I'm sorry I forgot them yesterday."

Maura nodded. "Mating later?" she asked hopefully.

"Definitely. Definitely later," he promised, his mind already imagining later that evening. He might need to take a cold shower. "But, for now, I need to get cleaned up and have breakfast before I start on these calls and emails. I'll be down in fifteen or twenty minutes."

He looked at Maura, who looked back at him with her dark, shining eyes and hair splayed on the pillows. It was all he could do not to climb back into bed with her and forget work for the day.

He gave an involuntary groan.

"Look," he said, "Here's a bra, panties, some sweatpants, and a shirt to put on after your shower. I can help you." He said this reluctantly, as he would rather get Maura out of her clothes than help her put them on.

It was hard to turn away from her, but he did. He went upstairs to shower, shave, and look professional in his button-down shirt and khaki pants.

When he returned to Maura, she bathed and put on underwear and sweatpants. She held the bra in her hand, looking confused. Rory had to hide a smile and explain what a bra was used for. He helped her put it on. She looked quite unhappy.

"This is what human females do?" she asked more than once.

Rory nodded. "I can help you fasten it."

She grimaced at the constricting thing and tugged a little at the bra. She sighed heavily after it was fastened. Again, his thoughts went to releasing the bra and her breasts for him to enjoy. He shook his head. He needed to focus. He motioned for Maura to follow him to the kitchen. He modeled scrambling eggs in the microwave and showed her how the toaster worked.

He ate quickly and apologized to Maura. "I need to get upstairs, sorry," he said. "Come up when you're ready, but please be quiet, as I'll likely be on the phone. Maybe you can sketch?"

13

MAURA

$\mathcal{M}$aura chewed thoughtfully at the remainder of her breakfast, thinking about the difference between the Rory of earlier this morning with their mating and the Rory rushing upstairs for his work. He was distracted and worried. Maura wished she could help, but she wasn't sure what she could do.

She abandoned her breakfast and gave her remaining bite of toast to a waiting and drooling Skipper. As she had seen Rory do, she rinsed off her plate and put it in the machine next to the sink.

She walked up the stairs carefully and quietly as she heard Rory's frustration ebb and flow in his conversation. She tiptoed into his office, gave a little wave, picked up the drawing paper and pencils pad, and exited. She wondered where to go.

She remembered the small, sunny room at the end of the hallway. It was perfect. She loved the light in the room, like captured sunshine. She settled on the couch and placed the pencils and an eraser on a small end table beside her. Opening the pad of drawing paper, she lost herself in her artwork.

A couple of hours later, she felt Rory's presence before she saw him. He hovered in the doorway, watching her for a couple of minutes before he greeted her and pulled her out of her latest drawing.

She looked up from the papers spread around her rather shyly, "Hi."

He looked stressed. His blue eyes looked duller than she had seen them, and his glance had a worried edge. He tugged a little at his hair before shoving his hands into his pockets. But his smile was just for her, and his glance filled her with desire for him.

"Hi yourself," he greeted. "You've been busy." He gestured at the artwork strewn around her. "May I see?"

"Of course, just don't judge too harshly."

She twisted her hands nervously as Rory looked at the drawings. She wondered what he would say and watched his expressions carefully. He studied the artwork – carefully. She wasn't surprised at this. He seemed to be a careful and thoughtful man. The drawings were intricate mandalas and patterns similar to Celtic knots, but they were created with beautifully drawn shells, driftwood, seaweed, and rocks. He told her in an awed voice that he had never seen anything like this, telling her that her shading with the pencils made the pictures photorealistic, and even in black and white, they nearly jumped off the page. She blushed at his praise.

"These are incredible, Maura," he said in awe. "You could sell these or put the designs on things. I think people would love these. You really have something here."

"Sell them?" Maura questioned.

"Yes, at galleries and gift shops."

"I don't know what you're talking about," Maura admitted.

"Well, maybe I can take you to a gallery or two later this week, and you can see what they're like. Other artists put their paintings and sculptures in galleries to sell. Photographs too. As we discussed this morning, I need to grab a quick lunch and head to the job site."

"Things are going well?" she asked.

Rory grimaced, "Not like I would like them to, but perhaps we can salvage the situation. I need to make nice with this contractor and get him to finish the job in a timely fashion. He doesn't see things from my perspective or the owners' perspective. He goes to the beat of his own drum."

Maura was puzzled by his language. She didn't know what he was talking about, but he was hurrying to leave, so she didn't say anything. His language didn't make sense to her, and she didn't know what he was talking about. She held in a sigh of frustration. She wished Rory were staying at home. Instead, she stacked the drawings neatly on the desk.

"I'll also pick up more drawing paper when I look for shoes, okay?"

Maura flashed him a brilliant smile. "That would be lovely. I am catching up on years and years' worth of drawing time. I can't stop."

"I can see that," Rory added with a smile.

He gave her a soft kiss. She returned it, putting her arms around his neck and pressing against him.

He groaned, "Lunch and work. I need to focus on that, or I will spend the afternoon in bed with you."

"Another plan for another day," she commented, pulling away reluctantly.

"Absolutely," Rory assured her.

Skipper, who had spent the morning in a puddle of sunshine, looked at them and barked. This broke the sexual tension humming between Rory and Maura, and they both laughed.

"Yes, Skipper, outside for you and lunch for us," Rory told the dog.

Rory asked Maura to take Skipper outside while he made lunch. Maura did, relishing the sea breeze and breathing in the salty air. The sea called to her, but surprisingly, she did not want to race inside and put on her pelt. She felt content and turned her face to the sun high in the sky. Drawing had settled her. It gave her a sense of peace and was like a warm current of water coursing through her body.

Skipper did his business and approached her. She bent down to pat and kiss him on the head before returning to the kitchen.

Like breakfast, Rory intended to eat quickly and get out the door. He didn't speak much but downed a sandwich and grabbed a handful of chips before giving her a perfunctory kiss, saying, "I'll see you later."

Maura, mid-way through half a sandwich, looked up, surprised. "All right, see you later."

And he was gone. Instantly, the house seemed emptier. She sighs out loud this time. Maura looks at Skipper. She is glad the dog is there. Maura supposes it is the herd mentality. She is used to having seals around her all the time. Being alone is nice occasionally, but she always likes the presence of others near her. Even when she is inside herself, creating the sand paintings, she always has the presence of the other Selkis and seals nearby.

"It's just you and me, Skipper."

He thumped his tail and looked hopefully at the piece of sandwich in her hand. Maura laughed and gave it to him.

"Let's go upstairs and draw some more, but first, I need to get something."

Maura picked up her pelt from the bedroom and took it upstairs to the little room she used as a studio. There was a closet. Maura opened it and laid the pelt gently on the floor, patting the head before she closed the door.

There, that's done. It's safe, she thought.

It surprised her that Skipper did not find the pelt an unusual object. He didn't bark at it but accepted it as part of Maura. She liked that and kissed the dog on top of his head. Skipper wagged his tail.

Maura settled into her spot on the couch. Glancing at the stack of designs on the desk, she wanted to try something else. Skipper curled into the other corner of the couch. Could she draw him?

With hesitant strokes, she created the image of Skipper asleep on the couch. It took a while, but she was able to capture his essence in the drawing. Then she began to think about and draw her grandmother, mother, sisters, and other seals. It took her the better part of the afternoon, but her efforts were rewarded with clear, graphite images of her family.

Next, she tried her hand at drawing Rory. She realized she remembered a plethora of emotions and expressions with him, but she wasn't sure what to focus on. Drawing him only made her desire him more.

She put down her pencil and paper. Now, she was restless. Skipper looked up at her. She went downstairs and paced in front of the living room windows, occasionally glancing at the ocean.

Time. She didn't know what time it was or when he would return, but she desired him. He said late in the afternoon. That meant when the sun had turned towards the western horizon. It wasn't there yet, and it was midway between the noonday sun and sunset. She went back upstairs to his room. At least, if she was in his bed, she could pick up on some of his essence and energy.

She climbed in under the covers, sighing at the scent of Rory and feeling the vestiges of his energy. Something was blocking it. The clothes. She tore them off and threw them in a heap on the floor.

Without the clothing, she could feel Rory's essence and energy more closely. Her body thrummed with wanting. She reached up to brush her hair from her eyes and accidentally brushed a hand over her breast. Her desire for him was great, and the lightest touch made her nipple erect. She remembered him licking and sucking her breasts that morning and nearly groaned at the memory. She rubbed her hands on her breasts, focusing on the nipples and giving in to the pleasure it gave her.

It wasn't the same as Rory touching her, but it felt good. Her hands traveled south. She had never explored her human parts before. It had been a surprise at the pleasure they brought. She patted the mound near her clitoris, which was now swollen with excitement. She patted more, sending small jolts of pleasure through her. Wanting more, Maura took a finger and touched that small pearl and cried out at how it filled her body with the liquid fire she enjoyed with Rory's touch. She was astonished she could bring this pleasure to herself, and she continued to move her finger to give herself even more pleasure, climaxing after a few minutes.

She still wanted more. With her other hand, she worked to put her finger inside of her. It wasn't Rory. She wanted Rory, but she was able to bring herself to orgasm and, afterward, lay panting on the bed for a few minutes. She discovered the wonder of self-pleasuring and brought herself to yet another orgasm, imagining Rory inside of her.

14

RORY

Rory had had a day. He was a very patient man with a slow burn to anger. He had waited several months for this contractor to finish his portion of the job, and there didn't seem to be an end.

He approached the contractor this morning.

"Hey, Tom. How's it going?" Rory asked.

Tom grunted in return as he focused on measuring and cutting tile.

"Tom, when can we expect you to complete this? I'm getting heat from all around. You're months behind on the job. What's happening?" Rory tried to keep his voice even.

"Well..." Tom drawled, "My kid's been sick. I've been sick. It's been a shitshow at home, Rory."

"Then why didn't you tell us? Not communicating with us isn't helping. I've been keeping the bigwigs from firing you. You're not communicating with us at all," Rory's voice raised in frustration. He couldn't help it.

"From what they're saying, you're working other jobs while you leave us hanging. I'm almost inclined to believe it myself since you're only working part-time on this job."

"Now, just a cotton-picking minute," Tom began. He stopped measuring the tile and gripped the pencil and ruler in his hand. "You don't have any right to unload on me like that."

"I'm trying to save your job," Rory insisted.

"Jesus! I'm doing the best I can," Tom expostulated. "I'm not working another job."

"Are you sure? Is it something else? You've got to come clean, man," Rory told him. "I love your work. I want to recommend you for other jobs, but at this point, you will get fired."

Tom shook his head in disgust. "You just don't understand."

"So, what's the problem?" Rory asked. "Make me understand, Tom."

From what Rory could surmise, he worked only part-time. When he approached the man, excuse after excuse ensued, and he even turned the tables, stating that Rory was being unreasonable when Rory accused him of potentially working on another job since he only worked part-time on this job site. Rory did his best not to blow up at the man. He did excellent work, and didn't want him to leave before completing the job. He had to figure out a better way. At this point, he didn't know what that was. Could he play to the guy's ego? Pay him extra? He would need to think about it. Rory wanted to end this conflict and conversation. He wanted to get home to Maura. He imagined her in his house, sitting on the couch, waiting for him so they could mate, as she put it. He wanted to mate with her again and this was quickly turning into the longest day ever.

Tom made a disgusted sound and left. Rory shook himself out of his daydream and realized Tom was walking away.

"Hey!" he called after him. "Where are you going?"

"Later," Tom called over his shoulder and gave him a terse wave.

And that was that. Tom was a strange guy. Any conflict or confrontation and he ran for the hills. Rory knew he was gone for the day. So, it was time to go home, except he had promised her shoes and needed to keep that promise. He had checked the comparisons of men's to women's shoe sizes. He hoped he was correct that Maura would need a size eleven shoe with her extraordinarily long toes.

He found a paltry number of shoes in her size at the store. There were sneakers, but he wasn't confident Maura could tie them, and his time was limited with the recent developments with the contractor. He found a pair of flats and fuzzy slippers. That was all. They would have to wait until he could take her to a shoe store, likely on the weekend.

As he walked towards the registers, Rory passed the arts and crafts section of the store. On a whim, he went down the aisle and picked up a pad of drawing paper and a set of watercolors, acrylics, brushes, canvas, and watercolor paper. He wondered what Maura would think of these supplies. He could only imagine her beautiful drawings in full color. He was in awe of her talent. He grinned. He knew she would love it.

He was anxious to get home, and his need for Maura became almost overwhelming. He wanted to see, touch, taste, smell, and hold her like he was never letting go. He left the store and pressed his foot more firmly on the gas pedal to race home to Maura.

When he arrived at his house, it was quiet. Skipper ran up to him, tail wagging, but Maura didn't come to greet him. He looked in the guest bedroom and saw the sealskin no longer lying on the floor.

His gut clenched. *No*, he thought. *It couldn't be. Not after...*and he thought of their incredible lovemaking. What could he do? If she was gone, she was gone. Frantically, he dropped the shoes in the guest room and searched the first floor of the house, looking for Maura. Each room was empty. He flew up the stairs and headed to the small room she used as a studio. She wasn't there either. He would head to look on the beach when he dropped the art supplies on the desk. He stopped when he looked at the drawings, mesmerized by what he saw. They were drawings of seals and the drawings of Selkis. He wondered who they were.

Rory turned out of the room and entered his bedroom in a daze. He couldn't believe she was gone. Were the drawings a message? Were they a goodbye? He wondered if she left them as a gift and returned to the sea. He rubbed his face and could feel tears pricking at the edges of his eyes. He felt hollow inside and a little sick. It was then he noticed Maura in his bed. Relief washed over him. She was here! She hadn't gone back to the sea. His tense shoulders relaxed, and his ragged emotions calmed.

There she was, so very beautiful. He stared at her hair spread around her, and she was playing with herself, her eyes tightly closed in ecstasy. Her nipples were erect, peeping out of the coverlet. She was arching her hips up. He found it incredibly sexy to watch her, and he couldn't resist going over to her.

His hand lightly brushed her breast, and her eyes flew open. When they focused, and she saw him, her eyes grew deeper with longing.

"Please," she mouthed to Rory. "Please."

Rory didn't hesitate. He removed his clothing in under a minute, and she opened her arms to him, moaning with relief when he lay on top of her, her soft curves beneath him. He wanted to sink into her and meld their skin together.

Maura's earlier playtime left her a puddle of wetness for Rory. He took full advantage and worked to bring her to more orgasms. Rory took his one hand and held both her wrists above her head. His other hand massaged one breast while he gave the other a tongue assault until she writhed beneath him, begging him to enter her. He obliged.

She climaxed multiple times, moaning and, one time, screaming, "Oh, Sedna!"

They lay side by side after their love-making, Rory propped up on one elbow and his arm lightly across her.

"Oh, God, Maura!" Rory's voice was crowded with emotion. "You are..." The jumble of emotions nearly overwhelmed him, surpassing his ability to speak. His desire for Maura eclipsed anything he had ever felt for another woman. She was sweet, innocent, and sexy. She was addictive, and he seemed to ache for her constantly. She was the piece that made him whole, but could he tell her that? And how? His voice trailed off.

Instead of speaking, he took his hand and ran one finger that traced her jawline. Then, he took his hand and cupped her face gently.

Maura smiled up at him, now drowsy and happy from their lovemaking. His breath caught in his throat. She was stunning.

And so, he told her in a fervent whisper, "You are so beautiful."

15

MAURA

Maura was floating on the hazy sea of post-orgasm. Her body felt as light as air, and her brain was a pleasant mush of happiness. She barely heard Rory's words, but they spoke to her heart.

He was falling asleep. She extricated herself from Rory and went into the tiled room – the bathroom, Rory called it. There, she saw her reflection. She stood, looking at herself. She wasn't used to seeing her reflection. It hadn't been possible as a seal. As a human, they danced on the beach and occasionally looked at themselves in still rock pools. But Maura had no idea of beauty and what beautiful meant. She admired her sister Kelsi's lighter and redder hair. She also envied her sister Rhona's slim and graceful body. She always felt small and squat. She looked at herself with different eyes now. Rory liked what he saw. That made her stand a little straighter and as tall as her petite stature would allow. Her hair was messy, and she didn't think it was beautiful. She didn't mind the curves of her body. It was just her, and she was glad Rory enjoyed what he saw and touched.

Maura turned and saw the little pool of a bathtub. She filled it and climbed in, soaking in the warmth for a few minutes before scooting underwater and getting her long hair completely wet. She saw some soap on the side of the tub, so she scrubbed her hair and body, rinsing thoroughly before soaking until the water cooled.

Feeling much better, she stood, dripping on the bathroom mat. She didn't feel the need for a towel. She searched the drawer for a comb and was happy to find a wide-toothed one. It reminded her of a comb her grandmother had, carved of wood with intricate design. This one was brilliant green in color and made of plastic. She wrung out her hair with her hands over the tub, sat on the edge, looked out at the ocean, and began to comb the tangles out of her hair.

She gazed at the darkening sea and sky. It was windy tonight. Maura could see white caps adorning waves like jewelry as far as she could see. She shivered. She wondered how the herd was doing and if she had any family left. It was a sobering thought about all the seal lives taken with the sickness. And who was left in the herd? Did they make it to New Jersey, where humans helped sick seals? She ached for her family. She would be forever haunted by the look in her mother's eyes when she was so very ill and knew the end was coming. Her sister Rhona disappeared somewhere North of Boston. Maura wondered if she was alive. Did she survive the virus? She missed Rhona's sunny disposition, sense of play, and camaraderie. Maura had wanted to swim to New Jersey, where Kelsi supposedly was. She thought a lot about Kelsi. She heard she was with a human and wondered how she was faring in the human world. Kelsi was innocent and sweet. Maura had felt so lucky to have a great relationship with her sisters. She knew of others who sniped at one another and were jealous of each other. Maura felt fortunate that they loved one another and liked each other too. She remembered wistfully playing hide and seek in the kelp forests and dancing in the moonlight on the beach to the music of the waves and wind and the tunes Kelsi created.

She thought of the sea and its freedom. She loved torpedoing through the water, exploring new places, and playing in the kelp forests. It was a life of survival but also one of discovery. The ocean's diversity brought a sense of wonder over and over again. Could she find that sense of curiosity and wonder on land? She felt heartsick, torn between wanting Rory and wanting to return to her ocean life.

Her thoughts circled back to herself. Life with Rory was something she could never have imagined. Her life as a seal seemed almost foreign. Rory filled her heart, her mind, and her senses. To have someone fill the empty spaces inside of her was a new sensation for Maura. Was this love? Her mother, grandmother, and aunts talked of love and how human men would love Selkis but also keep them prisoner. They didn't have happy stories of Selkis interacting as humans. The Selki was always unhappy and tried to find a way back to the sea. Rory wasn't keeping her prisoner. She felt she imprisoned herself by her need to be near him and her desire to mate with him. And was that wrong? Should she return to the sea and her seal life? She glanced in the direction where her pelt lay in the closet. At this moment, she didn't want to return to the sea.

Skipper came into the bathroom and leaned against Maura's legs. She scrubbed at his ears, and he elicited a doggy moan of happiness. He put a paw on her leg and looked up at her. He needed to go outside.

"All right, Skipper. I need to get some clothes on. My pelt won't do," she told the dog.

Skipper looked up at her as if she understood and pawed at her again.

"Okay, boy," she repeated the words she heard Rory say.

Night had fallen completely when she and Skipper went outside. Clouds blotted out the myriad of stars. A cold breeze whipped around her. Down the stairs to the beach, the ocean crashed, whooshed, and sounded like a thousand voices whispering to her to return to the sea. The sea was a living, breathing creature with communities of several creatures within. They all called to Maura to return to the sea. It was like a whispering claxon or siren's song. Her body turned automatically towards the sound, and she walked almost mindlessly to the steps.

Skipper raced over and put a cold nose into her palm, waking her from a daze. The sound of a door slamming reverberated in the periphery of her consciousness. It was only a moment until Rory was beside her.

What had she been about to do? Was she going to listen to the sea and return without her pelt? How crazy was that?

"Hi," Rory said, putting an arm around her. He looked at her expression as best he could in the night. Whatever he saw or sensed bothered him. "Are you all right?" he asked.

Maura leaned into him, relishing his closeness, feeling those empty spaces fill within her with the emotions she felt for Rory.

"I am now," she told him.

He pulled back and looked at her quizzically.

Skipper circled by their feet and barked. Maura laughed.

"Let's go in," she said.

16

RORY

Rory put his arm around her, and Maura leaned into him. She had been trance-like when he approached her earlier, so he questioned her, "What was going on there, Maura? You seemed to be in a trance."

Maura stopped and pulled away from him before answering, "The ocean and all of its creatures were calling me to return," she said.

His glance was worried, "And?"

"I don't know," she answered honestly.

Rory wasn't sure how to feel or what to do. Just over two hours ago, he thought this life with Maura had ended when he couldn't find her pelt. His despair was a new emotion for him. He wasn't sure he wanted to or if he could live without Maura now. Even after only a few days, she was part of him and part of his life. He had no idea where this relationship would lead.

And there it was. It was so different from his other relationships with women. Most of his relationships weren't serious. Only one stung him badly when she jilted him after proposing. He had thought Melanie had been 'the one.' Instead, he was more of a joke to her. It still hurt. And he hadn't dated since, despite the cajoling of friends and his mom. *She* wanted grandchildren and made no bones about it in conversation. He teased her that she should have been a matchmaker the way she worked to fix him up with various 'acceptable' women in her eyes.

But how could he trust Maura when she openly stated she wasn't sure if she wanted to stay or return to the sea? This love and lust thing with Maura – he wished he hadn't fallen so hard or so fast. What if she did leave? He didn't think he could handle it.

And who could he talk with about it? Lizzie, his best friend since second grade, was in Cape May with her wife for a romantic getaway. Lizzie always judged his romantic relationships. She abhorred Melanie and always had something to say about the women in his life. He wondered what she would think of Maura. He didn't want to interrupt Lizzie and Jo's romantic getaway, so he didn't text, and he wouldn't call.

They went inside and sat silently on the couch, staring at the dark waves with lacy caps. Skipper curled up at their feet. The silence was uncomfortable.

Finally, Rory asked, "What do you mean by 'you don't know?'

He shifted uncomfortably on the couch and waited for Maura's answer.

Maura's face contorted with conflicting emotions. She twisted her hands in her lap, taking a few minutes to look into Rory's eyes.

She responded quietly, almost whispering, "I said, 'I don't know,' because I have never been in human shape this long. What will happen to me here? Do you want me to stay? I don't know about the human world. But I also don't know if I want to return to being a seal. Being with you..." She flushed. "I've never known anything like this."

She stopped. He gazed at her and nodded in understanding.

"I feel the same. I have never experienced anything like this," he admitted.

Maura looked relieved, and Rory gave a sigh of relief, the tension draining from him.

Then, he looked puzzled and asked, "What happened to your pelt? When I came home and didn't see it in the downstairs bedroom, I thought..." Rory swallowed. "I thought you had left, and my world was ending."

"Oh! Oh!" Maura cried. She scooted over to him and curled right into his arms.

Rory dropped a kiss on her head and curled his arm around her. She felt so good in his arms.

She turned in his arms and looked up at him. "I put my pelt in the closet where I draw. Is that okay?"

"It's fine," he assured her. "In fact, I brought you some presents. They're in the drawing room." He chuckled.

She didn't understand the joke and asked, "What's so funny?"

Rory thought about it. There was no way she would have any perspective about drawing rooms in ages past. Maura was very literal in language.

Instead, he gently moved her away and took her hand as he stood up from the couch.

"Come on," he said. "Let me show you what I picked up for you."

Mystified, Maura followed him up the stairs. Rory stood, grinning proudly at the things on the desk. Maura went to investigate. She touched the drawing pads, canvas, paints, and pencils.

"I don't know what all of this is," she admitted.

Rory explained that watercolors and acrylics would add color to her drawings.

"They both clean up with water," he told her. "Let me get you some, and I'll show you."

Rory went to get water while Maura went to the couch to pet Skipper. Soon, Rory returned with a jar of water. He demonstrated how to paint and mix colors to create other colors. Maura was agog when Rory showed her how to mix two colors to make a third. She never dreamed this could happen. She never had tools like this. Her fingers itched, wanting to take the brush from Rory's hand and begin playing with the colors.

Rory turned to her and grinned when he heard her suck in a breath of excitement. "Go for it," he told her, handing her the brush.

He watched as she tentatively took the brush and dipped it into the watercolor. She made a large swathe of cerulean blue across the paper and was amazed at the gradience from solid color to wash. Next, she mixed red and blue in the small palette Rory had bought and created a purple to add to the blue.

"This is incredible!" she told Rory in awe.

"I think you're going to have fun," Rory stated. "You can paint to your heart's content while I work."

He looked at her other drawings and picked up the one with her mother, grandmother, and sisters. "Who's this?" he asked.

Maura stilled. "That's my family." She pointed to each and named them. "My grandmother and mother are gone," she told him. "Kelsi is in New Jersey. I believe she is living with a human. My sister Rhona..." she trailed off. Tears filled her eyes. "I don't know if she is alive or dead."

Rory took this in. How sad for Maura. He wondered how she knew about her sister Kelsi. He looked upset and wondered if he should wait to talk to her. But he wanted to know.

"How do you know your sister Kelsi is in New Jersey?"

Startled, Maura turned to look at him. Finally, she stated clearly, almost as if he were simple, that seals have a language and a communication network like humans. Now, it was his turn to look startled. He had never pondered on the way animals communicate. He stared.

"We sort of have a network where seals share the news about other seals, good fishing grounds, and safe places to haul out," she explained.

"What about you?" she asked.

"My dad is gone. I don't have any brothers or sisters. My mom is in the city."

"City?"

"New York," Rory answered.

"Oh," Maura answered, not quite understanding.

"We'll go some time," Rory promised. "You will be amazed. And I think you would like my mom."

"Tell me about your mother."

Rory paused, thinking before answering, "She's tall. Very tall and Scandinavian-looking. Her very blond hair has turned snowy white in the last year or so. She's elegant and has a good sense of humor. She works in publishing in the city."

Maura nodded, remembering the photographs she had seen. "Publishing?" Maura asked, not understanding the term.

"Making books. She's an editor," Rory explained, "of these." And he pulled a book off a small bookcase in the room.

When he opened the book, Maura could only see odd designs and squiggles. She looked up at Rory.

"These shapes on these lines, do they have meaning?" she asked.

Startled and not considering Maura was illiterate, he answered, "Yes.

This is the written foundation of our language. We read for information and entertainment. It's difficult to get by in the human world without knowing how to read."

"Oh," Maura said softly, her voice small. "I guess if I want to stay as a human, I'll need to learn to read?"

"Most definitely, and you will need to learn to write," Rory confirmed. "I don't know how to accomplish that. I'll have to research or see if there are classes somewhere. I'll check on that tomorrow."

Rory tugged at his hair. Near panic washed over him quickly. What else would Maura need to know? Do? She didn't have any identification. How could they manage that? It was like having a toddler in an adult body. She didn't know how to live or to cope in the human world without guidance. No wonder some of the Selkis who lived on land were unhappy. There were so many people out there who could take advantage of them. People could be ugly. But what about him? Was it fair that he was nearly Pygmalion and she, Galatea, teaching her about the human world? He felt that he needed to be a little careful of Maura and definitely gentle as she maneuvered through this new life she had chosen.

Oblivious to his roiling thoughts, Maura stated happily, "I can hardly wait to paint!"

"Yes, while you paint," he agreed.

17

MAURA

Rory held her gently that night. They spooned together, and Maura was sandwiched between Rory and Skipper. But she couldn't sleep. Her brain wouldn't turn off with all the images she wanted to paint the next day, and she also felt a trifle overwhelmed about learning to read. There was so much she didn't know about in the human world. She wondered again if she should stay as a human or return to the sea as a seal. Being a seal wasn't as complicated. It was all about survival—finding food, a place to rest, and avoiding sharks and other predators. Being a Selki, she could escape that to dance joyfully with her family on various beaches. That had been the extent of her humanity. Even though she had seen humans on the shore, she hadn't paid attention to the clothing or actions. She observed, occasionally wondering how they lived their lives, but truly, she hadn't given it much thought. As a seal, she needed to survive; that was her focus as she observed from the sea.

Maura gently pushed Skipper to move him. He groaned in protest but jumped from the bed and looked at her. She couldn't laugh. She didn't want to wake Rory. Carefully, she extricated herself from his arms and padded barefoot down the hallway to her drawing room. Skipper followed her, jumping on the couch and circling three times before settling down. He went back to sleep immediately.

Maura took one of the books off the shelf, sat with Skipper, and opened it. This book had lovely illustrations. She looked at the black shapes on the pages. How would she ever make sense of this? She wondered if she could learn this written language. Sighing, she returned the book to the shelf, wondering about other things she needed to learn.

Maura also wondered about Rory's mother. Would she like Maura and approve of her mating with Rory? It was another worry.

She looked at the art supplies. How kind of Rory to think of her and purchase supplies to create art. She stood up and went to the desk where they lay. She would need to do painting sitting at the desk, not curled up on the couch with Skipper.

Maura wanted to try painting with watercolors, not wanting to wait until morning She filled the jar with water for the brushes and opened the paints, admiring the little blocks of solid paint. She spent a little time mixing on the palette as she planned the painting in her head. This would be a quick experiment. Maura started to add color, creating an ocean scene with waves crashing on the shore. She loved the color and added swathes of coral and peach as if the sun was rising. Instinctively, Maura knew she had to let the paper dry to create the layers of color. Impatient to create more, she took another piece of paper and started to sketch a seal, peeping out between strands of kelp. This scene had more depth of color, and she became lost in the underwater world as she painted. After painting for a couple of hours, her eyes became gritty with fatigue and her focus waned. She yawned.

Reluctantly, she stood, yawning again, and took her brushes to the bathroom to rinse off. Skipper followed her like her shadow. Maura crawled into bed and snuggled against Rory. The night was chilly, and she had neglected to put on the slippers Rory had bought. Her feet felt like the icy waters of the North Atlantic. Rory put his arm around her and automatically cupped her breast. She sighed contentedly as Skipper joined them and lay on her feet, warming them. She was asleep in seconds, dreaming of things to paint.

18

RORY

Rory's alarm pulled him from sleep. He had been dreaming of Maura and making love to her. And, here she was, in his arms. He smiled and thought of waking her. But he was surprised she hadn't woken with the alarm and his movements. She was dead asleep. He didn't feel he could wake her for lovemaking if she was so fatigued, thinking she was still recuperating from her illness. Skipper seemed tired, too, opening one eye and looking at Rory briefly before stretching his legs and returning to sleep.

Odd, Rory thought—very odd. He shrugged his shoulders and went into the bathroom. There, he noticed watercolor brushes on the sink. Maura must have painted during the night, he thought. He left the bathroom to investigate.

Sure enough, on the desk in what he coined the 'drawing room' lay two watercolors curling up at the edges. They were magnificent. She had captured dawn on the ocean with just a few strokes, and the water had such layered depth with the color. The other painting, of a seal peeking out between strands of kelp, was just as beautiful. Maura could sell these. Tourists coming to the beach would snap them up. He wondered if there was a gallery that would take her paintings. She would need to sign them. Maybe he could teach her how to write the letter "M" for Maura Muir. That would be an easy start – "MM" and add the year.

Her paper curled. He would need to teach her how to tape her paper to a Masonite board to keep it from curling.

He went downstairs to make himself coffee and mull over how to get Maura's art into a gallery. If that could be accomplished, she would be more independent. With her name 'out there' as a human, it would give more credence to her existence. If she could justify her life in Long Island with her work at galleries, it might be slightly easier to show residency and a need to live in the States and obtain identification. At least, he hoped so. While his coffee brewed, he searched for galleries in the area. He was sure his mom would know of some galleries in New York, too. She and her cronies regularly went to gallery openings. Her home and office were filled with beautiful pieces of art and sculpture. His mom's favorite hangouts were the art museums in the city.

He sat with his coffee and looked at the gallery choices. Perhaps he could take Maura this weekend. She would probably like that. There were a few in the area. One was near the local aquarium. He wondered what Maura would think of fish being captured in tanks. He knew there were seals there as well. That may or may not be a good choice for her to visit.

He thought it would be good to take photos of her artwork so that he could share them with the gallery owners. That would be a start, at least. And, to teach Maura how to write the letter, "M."

He glanced at the time. He had projects to work on and people to call. He returned upstairs. Maura was still dead asleep. Rory showered and dressed. He knew some people worked at home in their pajamas, but he couldn't do that. Especially if he had to fly out the door to head to a job site to help solve a problem.

His stomach growled. He hadn't eaten yet, thinking of waiting for Maura before he breakfasted. He would need a second cup of coffee and a snack, so Rory returned to the kitchen to do just that before heading to his office.

He checked his email and reviewed a couple of potential upcoming jobs. One was to design a house on the island. The ideas looked sound, and he returned the email to the potential customer and attached an estimate for his work.

His phone buzzed with an incoming text. He read it and groaned. The contractor hadn't shown up as expected. Rory knew he had a habit of waiting until mid-morning to show. He didn't understand why, but that's how it was. He texted the crew manager back and asked him to stay patient. He also texted the contractor, asking when he would be onsite. They needed to finish this project.

Next, he went to his drafting table to sketch out a design. Before working on his CAD program, he played with it with a pencil, paper, and ruler.

After over an hour, he returned to the bedroom to check on Maura. She was beginning to wake up and smiled when she saw Rory before yawning deeply. She looked so sexy with her soft, sleepy eyes. The sheet just covered her bare nipple and the folds of the sheet molded around her body.

"Good morning, beautiful," he said, sitting perched on the edge of the bed near her and leaning over to kiss her.

Maura blushed prettily at the compliment. "Good morning."

"You slept in."

Maura looked up at Rory with a hint of concern. "Is that a problem?"

"No, of course not," he insisted. "It was just a comment."

"Oh. I, uh, I couldn't sleep. I was so excited to paint that I got up to try my hand at it," Maura confessed.

"I saw. They're amazing. I love the seal peeking through the kelp," he told her, asking, "Are you hungry?"

Maura nodded.

He stood up. "Let's eat breakfast together. Afterward, I can show you how to tape your paintings so they don't curl before I return to work."

She showed a long bit of leg getting out of bed, and it was all Rory could do not to stroke her leg up to her nether regions. He twitched in his pants as his stomach growled loudly. He ignored his desire to grab her, push her down onto the bed, and make love to her then and there. Instead, he suggested waffles this morning.

"I thought I would make a quick breakfast before I return to work. Are you hungry?" he asked her.

Maura nodded.

Rory modeled using the toaster to cook the waffles. He had Maura heat the second batch. Her delight at the sweet taste of maple syrup and the crunchy waffles made him smile.

After breakfast, he went to the shed to find some pieces of wood while Maura changed from her night clothes. He brought in three that would be convenient for her to use for her paintings. He took them to the drawing room and waited for Maura so that he could show her how to tape the watercolor paper to the boards.

Maura couldn't wait to begin painting again. Rory's idea of taping down the paintings was extremely helpful. She mulled over colors, rubbing a finger over her chin while she decided. The palette was empty, and Maura mixed one color after another until she found the shade she desired. She took a brush with bold strokes, dipped it into the paint, and, like magic, created a seascape. Rory planned to purchase Masonite boards online. He knew they would arrive in the next day or two and he told Maura this.

They fell into a comfortable rhythm. Maura rose with Rory, they breakfasted, and both got to work. Rory couldn't believe how prolific Maura was with her painting. The ideas seemed to pour from her fingers. He had her practice writing letters to spell, write, and sign her name. She was painterly in this fashion, too, and had a stylized MM for her signing her paintings. He was pleased and impressed at her progress.

"Maura," Rory spoke gently to her one morning. I think you should consider selling some of your drawings and paintings. Humans will appreciate their beauty and your perspective of ocean and beach life."

"Okay," she began slowly, "but I don't understand."

"A gallery is a place where artists display their work. People go to galleries when they

want to decorate their homes or give gifts. The money they spend on the artists' works helps the artists get more paints, canvases, and supplies."

Maura still looked puzzled.

"Look, I'll take you to a gallery this weekend, and then you can see for yourself."

Rory realized Maura didn't have a clue about money, jobs, making a living, or all of those economic things that ran their lives. He wondered how she would react when going into a store. It was going to be an interesting weekend.

19

MAURA

The human way of life fascinated Maura. She felt she was easing into it fairly well. Rory was very good at modeling how to do things. Rory showed her how to turn on the television. Most of the time, it wasn't easy to understand why the people did what they did. She liked the channel that had cooking. She thought she might like to try to make a meal soon. The other channel she liked did things with houses – like building and redecorating. She was fascinated with houses, and Rory made the plans for the building. She liked his 'house art' as she called it. He called it CAD or blueprints. She didn't know why. She also liked her way of art. Painting was a wonder! It brought her drawings into another dimension. She would lose herself in mixing and executing the colors on the paper. For now, she only played with the watercolors. She liked their transparency, the light they brought to the drawings and the color. She would try acrylics soon. Rory promised to show her a television channel where a man painted all day. He said he wanted to buy her the paints, brushes, and other supplies that went along with the program so she could paint alongside the man on the television.

Their lives fell into a nice rhythm. When Rory went to work, she went to work painting. Rory kept talking about selling her paintings for money. She didn't understand what that was. Maura was totally new to having others like her paintings and wanted to put them in their houses. Rory said he would need to get a gallery owner to agree to sell her paintings. She didn't know what that was either. This weekend, he promised. She wasn't sure what weekend meant. She knew the turn of the sun and the moon. Rory was teaching her about days and dates. He showed her a calendar and helped her count the days until the weekend when he didn't have to work as much. She had so much to learn.

After dinner they would take Skipper on a walk, usually on the beach. Being near the ocean was getting easier for Maura. It still called to her, but she often took Rory's elbow and leaned into him.

"What's it like?" he asked, "being a seal?"

Maura didn't answer immediately at first. Finally, she said, "It's survival, day to day. Every single day, you need to be safe, to find food, and to find a safe place to haul out and rest. You make life so easy here for me. You make me feel safe, Rory. I don't have to worry about sharks or how to find something to eat. I have a safe place to rest, too. It's quite a change from what I'm used to. But, I love it," she told him, reaching up to kiss his cheek.

Jealous, Skipper ran back and jumped up towards Maura.

"Oh! You! I love you too!" Maura crooned and scrubbed at Skipper's ears.

The dog pressed against her.

Rory was quiet for a while before answering, "Some people have to fight for their survival every day," he told her. "We're pretty lucky."

"Yes, aren't we lucky," Maura said softly. They stopped and looked out at the vast ocean for a few minutes before turning towards home.

And she did feel lucky. His comments gave her pause. Her mother, aunts, and grandmother all warned Maura and her sisters about the dangers of being with human men. According to the elder females, human men were greedy and abusive. They assured Maura and her sisters that no one could be happy with a human. The girls had grown up fearing humans, thinking men would steal their pelt and make them prisoners. She was so happy with Rory and glad he wasn't like that. She paused, wondering about her sister Kelsi. She was rumored to be with a human. For Kelsi's sake, she hoped the man was good, like Rory.

Marua picked up on the stress Rory was facing with his job. Some days, his eyes were filled with expressions of anger and worry. His face was more drawn, and he frequently tugged at his dark, curly hair.

Maura wanted to give Rory a bit of seal magic. consisting of the light carried within all creatures. As a selki, she could pull the light and energy from animals and the energy from humans. It was a powerful force from nature and from within that healed and gave comfort. When she touched Rory, she would close her eyes, pull the energy from the earth and the air, and send it pulsing through him. After a few moments, Rory didn't realize it, but he visibly relaxed. The seal magic filled his body with light, and there wasn't room for the negativity. It oozed out of him, and she brushed it away and into the air to dissipate. She didn't tell him about the light not yet but thought it eased his worries.

It was quiet in Rory's neighborhood with the people living at their other homes. She wondered about them and how noisy they would be when people returned to the shore in the summer. Rory told her stories of gathering called parties at the nearby residences. No one seemed to come down his street save for what Rory called the postal worker. Skipper didn't like the man and gave a low growl as soon as he heard the vehicle. He barked and barked when the postal worker came near the house. Rory ordered many packages, particularly things for Maura. So, Skipper had a hard time every afternoon when the postal worker and his vehicle came up the driveway to drop something off at the door. Maura hid in the other room, not wanting to meet this human that Skipper did not like.

So, it was a surprise when she was working in her studio and heard a voice shout, "Hey, Bro! I brought you saltwater taffy!"

Rory had gone to the job site, and Maura couldn't imagine who had come into the house. Skipper went to investigate, but Maura heard no barks or growls. Who could this be? She hoped Skipper was all right, so she went downstairs to investigate.

Walking into the kitchen, Maura found a woman petting and crooning to Skipper. She stopped, frozen at the doorway, staring at the tall young woman with extremely short, spiked hair. She recognized the woman from the photographs Rory had in the house. Rory mentioned her name, but Maura couldn't remember it. She was a good friend of Rory's. She wondered what this woman would think about her in Rory's house. She was nervous, but seeing Skipper obviously happy to see this woman, Maura relaxed a little, but only slightly.

She wasn't used to meeting human females outside of her Selki circle.

She stood, waiting, wondering what to say. The woman noticed her and stared at her in surprise.

Skipper eventually pulled away from the woman and sat beside Maura. When Skipper pulled away, the woman glanced up and noticed Maura standing there. She pulled back in obvious surprise. "Who are you?" she inquired, staring at Maura skeptically.

Maura noticed her glance was wary.

"I'm Maura. Who are you?"

"I'm Lizzie."

"Lizzie!" Maura exclaimed, now remembering the name. "I've heard so much about you!"

Lizzie gave a sardonic chuckle. "Well," she said, "that makes one of us. Who are you?"

Maura flushed and said, "I'm Maura. I – I'm here with Rory."

"Hmm," Lizzie replied. "He hasn't mentioned you."

"You were away with your wife when I arrived," Maura said, nervously pacing the kitchen. She didn't know what to do with her hands. They flapped a little, like when she was a seal and had flippers. Knowing this wouldn't be appropriate, she grasped them together tightly before continuing. "Rory talked about calling or texting you but didn't want to interrupt your vacation."

"Decent of him," Lizzie returned, with a sardonic note still in her voice. "When did you arrive? Where did you come from?"

The question didn't surprise Maura, but it did take her aback. Rory had discussed this with her. People would want to know where she came from and how she got there. It was going to be an issue. This was just the beginning. Lizzie looked suspicious. Perhaps that was a good thing. She obviously cared about Rory. Lizzie was a friend and wanted the best for him. Maura put herself in Lizzie's shoes – what if a strange seal from another herd came courting one of her sisters? What did she think of her sisters and human men? She hadn't pondered this beyond hoping Kelsi was with an understanding man and not with someone who kept her prisoner. Word through the herd was that she appeared to be very happy. She shook herself out of her thoughts, her pause being a hair too long, and answered Lizzie as truthfully as she could. The truth was always best, or as near truth as she could get. "I came about a week ago. Unfortunately, I was very ill when I arrived. I'm from the New Brunswick area."

"Canadian, eh?" Lizzie responded and then asked, "Where's Rory?"

"He's at his job site. I think he'll be returning soon. I don't know."

"I guess I should have texted or called first," Lizzie commented.

"Do you want to sit down and wait for him?" Maura asked.

"Okay. I can't stay too long," Lizzie told her as they entered the living room.

The women sat uncomfortably at either end of the long couch. Maura wasn't sure of what to say.

Finally, she asked, "How was Cape May?"

"It was beautiful," Lizzie answered, a dreamy look in her eyes. "They had everything decorated for the holidays."

"Holidays?" Maura asked.

Lizzie turned to Maura and gave her a sharp look. "Yes, the holidays."

Maura had seen a little bit on the television about the holidays. She wasn't sure what it was all about and meant to ask Rory. What could she say to Lizzie? She couldn't tell her she was a Selki and that seals don't celebrate the holidays. Her mind raced as she thought of an excuse.

"I'm sorry, I lived very remotely in New Brunswick. We didn't decorate for holidays," she ended lamely.

Skipper had been curled up on the couch between the two women. Suddenly, he jumped up and raced to the kitchen. Maura almost sighed with relief when she heard the door open. Rory.

2 0

RORY

Rory's mind was on the project and drove blindly on the familiar roads home. He slammed on the brakes when he pulled into the driveway, noticing Lizzie's car parked ahead of him. He very nearly hit Lizzie's car.

Lizzie. Shit. Lizzie was here, and that meant she met Maura. This could be a nightmare. He rushed into the house, nearly stumbling over Skipper.

The two women were in the living room, sitting at opposite ends of the couch. He looked at Maura and then at Lizzie. His awkward stance and expression amused Lizzie.

"Hey, bro," she greeted him.

"Hi," he responded weakly.

He dropped his knapsack near the doorway. Maura, with her huge brown eyes, was watching him. He gave her a swift kiss and went to Lizzie to hug her.

"I came over to drop off a box of Saltwater Taffy and was surprised to meet Maura," Lizzie her voice on the edge of sarcasm.

"Yeah, about that..." Rory started but trailed off.

"I mentioned that I just arrived from New Brunswick," Maura added helpfully.

"Uh, okay," he went on. He asked Lizzie, "Can I get you a beer or anything?"

"No thanks. It's my turn to make dinner, and I must stop at the store. I just dropped by to say hello," Lizzie said. "Walk me to my car?" she asked Rory before turning to Maura, saying, "Nice meeting you."

"Sure," he replied, already envisioning the conversation.

He glanced at Maura and followed Lizzie to her car.

When the door closed, she turned on him and said, "What the hell, man? Who is she? Where did you meet her? You only met her a few weeks ago, and she's moved in? Are you nuts?"

"Lizzie, cool it," Rory told her. "It's a long story."

"I'll bet," Lizzie replied. Her voice held the edge of something that Rory couldn't place. She was usually sarcastic, but her tone had a tinge of something else. Rory was too weary to think of what it was. He knew Lizzie, though, and knew she cared that he was all right.

"Can we talk about this later on?" he asked desperately. "I've had a hell of a day."

"Okay," Lizzie agreed, unlocking her car, "but this doesn't mean you're off the hook. Fess up, bro."

"And I love you too," he told her.

"Humph," Lizzie closed her car door.

He watched Lizzie maneuver out of his driveway and absently tugged at his hair. Lizzie's visit posed a problem. As Maura met other humans, they would want to know her story. They couldn't tell people she was a Selki. The reality of Maura needing a backstory niggled him, but he had ignored it while they were on their own little oasis in his house. The reality was crashing in, and Lizzie, he was sure, was the first of many inquiries. What would they do?

He went back into the house. Maura stood waiting for him in the kitchen, Skipper by her side. She looked worried.

He took her in his arms. She felt like home. He kissed her. And then, he kissed her ravenously, wanting to drink her in, pulling her to him with her hair like a silky pillow between his hands and her skin. He reached up under her sweatshirt and was pleased she wore no bra. He tweaked her nipples. She moaned in response. He loved that Maura wanted to be with him as much as he wanted to be with her.

Rory guided her to the living room in an awkward dance, making their way to the couch. He gently pulled her down and then pulled her sweat-shirt off so that he could have full access to her perfect breasts. He licked and kissed and twirled his tongue around the nipples. She arched her back, wanting him to take her entire breast in his mouth.

"Rory," she panted when he paused for a moment.

"Yes?" he inquired teasingly.

"More."

He complied. Her passion for him drove his passion on, and soon, they were all naked limbs entangled on the couch as the sun blazed its last goodbyes on the western horizon, lighting up the back windows with their golden and orange light strewn across the evening sky.

Afterward, they lay on the couch, Rory's face nestled in the hollow of Maura's neck. He breathed in her scent, relishing the breath of saltiness that always seemed to be with her. They were quiet for a long time.

Finally, Maura pushed him slightly away. Her deep, brown eyes were huge in her petite face. This was one of the moments he recognized the seal inside of Maura.

"Rory," her quiet tone exuded concern. "We have a problem."

"I know," he answered quietly.

He pushed himself up, gathered their clothes, and tucked a soft blanket over Maura. He then went upstairs and returned with their robes. They donned them and sat on the couch. She kept looking at him, but he wasn't sure, at first, what to say.

"We need to have a story about why you are here," he said eventually. "And we need to find a way to get paperwork that says you're legal to live here."

"I don't understand. Why can't I live with you?" she asked him.

Rory sighed and tugged at his dark hair and ran his hand over his face, scratching at the stubble beginning to grow on his cheeks. How to explain?

Finally, he said, "Our society, like your herd, has certain rules. One of them is that you belong here. We have documents – papers that state where we were born, numbers that identify us, addresses where we have lived. It's all tracked. You, being a seal, don't have any of this."

Maura mulled this over. She didn't know enough about the human world to comprehend everything needed to live as a human. Rory did.

And he seemed worried. So now, she was worried. How could she get these documents?

"We need to figure out why you came to the States," Rory said more aloud to himself than to Maura. "Why would you want to leave New Brunswick?"

"Looking for my sister, maybe?" Maura suggested. "I did get sick, and you took me in."

"That might work," Rory said. "Maybe you heard she was on an island, Long Island, to be specific, and you were taking a bus and stopping and looking for her." He paused. "And then someone stole your belongings. You were sick and delirious and didn't know what to do."

"And you came to my rescue," she added, snuggling against him.

"Yeah, a real knight in shining armor," Rory quipped.

"I don't know what that is," Maura said in a small voice. "Oh, Rory, I feel so stupid in the human world. I don't know anything about anything." She threw her hands out stiffly as if holding the weight of the world.

"But you're learning," he reassured her, putting his arm around her and drawing her close to the couch.

"We should eat something. You distracted me. Actually, Lizzie was the first distraction. Scrambled eggs?" he asked her.

"Sure," Maura agreed, "but let me try to cook them this time, okay?"

"Okay," Rory agreed.

MAURA

*R*ory hovered over Maura while she cooked. It made her nervous. She could do this. She asked Rory if he would toast the bread and butter the toast while she finished cooking.

Over dinner, Maura asked Rory about holidays.

Rory paused. "As a seal, do you have a special day to honor Sedna?"

Maura shook her head.

"Hmm." Rory played with the salt and pepper on the table. "At this time of year, we have celebrations. Historically, it refers to when the ancient peoples feared the shortening days. When the solstice arrived, they celebrated with light – with bonfires, food, and joy for the sun's light returning. This has been translated over and over through ages and cultures. Jesus Christ is celebrated at Christmas. He's sort of the male version of Sedna – the father of us all. He is said to be the 'light of the world.'"

Rory looked up to see if Maura understood. She was listening with interest. He went on, "Other cultures have light festivals as well. When we go out tomorrow, you'll see white and colored lights everywhere as darkness falls. It's also a time of gift-giving. People like to share their bounty and give gifts from the heart to loved ones. They also believe in a guy in a big red suit who gives presents to boys and girls here in the States. Other cultures have other gods and goddesses that bring presents." He paused before adding, "I think that's about it."

Maura tried to comprehend what Rory was telling her without looking too confused. The man in a red suit and a male counterpart to Sedna didn't make sense to her. She had nothing to compare it to in the Selki world. Regarding gifts, when they were in human form, often her family would gift each other a pretty shell or flower they found, but they did not have a house or hidey-hole to keep their treasures. This, too, was confusing.

Even more terrifying was navigating the human world tomorrow. Rory seemed convinced other humans would like her artwork. She didn't have any perspective on this either. The thought of meeting a lot of humans was intimidating. Since she didn't have experience interacting with other humans, she would need to take cues from Rory. She wondered if she should confess her fears to him.

Maura's nervousness increased the next morning after Rory helped her strap herself in his car. She didn't like the confinement of the seatbelt or the confines of the vehicle. It was only when he began to drive swiftly down the road that Maura felt more relaxed. She loved it when Rory drove fast. It was like when she torpedoed through the water as a seal. She watched the landscape fly past her in awe. This landscape was vastly different than the landscape of the sea. She could see some parallels as the trees at the edges of the road reminded her of the great kelp forests. Rory pointed out flowering bushes that made her think of the anemones and corals at the bottom of the ocean. There were so many buildings and other cars. It seemed to Maura that humans worked to conquer the natural world and nearly snuff out nature.

He drove her to what he described as a small hamlet. She did not know what that meant. She saw groupings of buildings. Rory pointed out various landmarks, restaurants, and a park along the bay. Most of the buildings looked older, some with visible, peeling paint, but it was more of a feeling of age. He parked at a small set of shops. Rory came around to open her door and help her with the seatbelt.

Maura stepped out of the car and looked around with wide eyes. She tried not to gape, but this was alien to her. She had only viewed houses and stores from the ocean, swimming with the herd. When Maura and her family hauled out to dance, it was usually in the middle of a full moon night on a deserted beach. She had never seen anything like this. Instead, she took Rory's hand and looked at him rather than at the overwhelming landscape surrounding her.

Rory led her to a store with paintings and a few pottery pieces in the window. They entered, and the scent of oil paint and canvas enveloped them.

The variety of paintings in the gallery astounded Maura. She didn't know where to look first. Her mouth hung open slightly. She put her hands to her mouth one or two times to silence a quiet "oh!" of delight. She examined the brush strokes on the watercolors and how the artist used the layers of color, saturating with wet on wet or with dry brush techniques. The paintings in the next section were vibrant splashes of color. There were no defined shapes, and Maura could feel the emotions and passions the artists used as they painted. She found it interesting.

Rory took her by her elbow and led her to one corner, suggesting she make a planned route around the store. She nodded vaguely. Her eyes were only for the paintings. Rory whispered in her ear that he would talk with the proprietor. Again, she nodded, acknowledging him, but not really listening. She tore her eyes from the paintings and glanced over at Rory. He spoke with a distinguished older man with a clipped white beard and fingers almost as long as hers. The man glanced in her direction briefly. Maura went back to studying the paintings on display.

Rory came up to her a few minutes later. He seemed bothered and took her by the elbow.

"Let's leave," he whispered.

"What's wrong?" Maura whispered back.

"Later," he muttered.

They left the shop and stood in the fresh air. There was a bite of winter in it now, and Maura wondered if they might have some snow.

"What's wrong?" she asked again.

"He's not interested in your paintings," Rory grumbled. "He claims he doesn't have the space right now."

"Okay," Maura said agreeably. She was nonplussed by the gallery owner's reaction, and Rory was more upset than she was.

"C'mon," he said, "I think you'll like this place."

He led her to a store decorated with small white lights. Maura was enchanted. Inside were books upon books and other items. Her hands skimmed across a table with a pile of books. Oh, how she wished she could read. These books held so much knowledge. She wished she could drink them in. There was a small table filled with sparkling jewelry. The sun caught the crystals on the jeweled bracelets, and they flashed delightfully like bubbles from wild surf on the beach. There was a shelf of soft clothing with writing on it and lovely scarves in a variety of patterns that graced a corner display. It was so pretty. She suddenly thought of her sisters and how they would love the treasures of this place. "We might be able to find some things here to help you read," he suggested when he led her to the children's section

Maura looked at the beautifully illustrated books, carefully turning pages and studying the artwork. At the same time, Rory went to speak to the proprietor, another petite woman with bright, friendly, kind eyes and short, curly dark hair. Maura liked her instantly, too.

They were deep in conversation, so Maura lost herself in the picture books on the display. Rory pointed out a display of books that explained the upcoming holiday. She couldn't read the words but gleaned from the pictures a little understanding of the upcoming holiday by studying the pictures.

Maura wandered around the rest of the bookstore. She liked the soft, hand-crocheted toys, the sparkly jewelry, and the pretty scarves that hung in intervals around the store. In one case, there were pieces of sea glass jewelry. Maura often searched for sea glass when she was in her human shape. She and her sisters would stash some away safely when they hauled onto a beach to dance in the moonlight. They always hoped they would return to the beach and find the sea glass they had stowed. Maura remembered her aunt calling the sea glass 'mermaid's tears,' telling of the legend that mermaids would cry when a sailor drowned. She almost scoffed aloud. Mermaids were not nice. They were likely the cause of the sailor's demise. They were tricky creatures.

Inside the case, something caught her eye. There was a ring with sea glass the same color as Rory's eyes. It was a rounded oval and well-frosted. It must have been in the ocean for a long time. She must have made a noise of delight because Rory approached her.

"What do you see?" he asked.

She pointed. "Look at that ring with the turquoise sea glass!" she breathed.

"You like it?" he asked her.

"Oh, yes! I love it."

"Maybe Santa Claus will bring it to you," he teased.

Maura looked blank, and Rory looked embarrassed.

"The man in the red suit that brings presents to good boys and girls," he explained. And then, in her ear, he whispered suggestively, "If you'll be a good girl, you might get a present."

A zip of electric tingling went through her at his suggestion. Her eyes widened with hope and pleasure.

She whispered, "You don't need to promise me a bauble for that."

Rory laughed.

"Back to business, I guess. The proprietor, Jazzlynn, suggested a few things about teaching children how to read in the parenting section. Let's check them out."

Maura followed Rory to another part of the store. These books were larger and had fewer pictures. She liked the art in the children's section. Rory leafed through a few books and chose two.

They came up to the counter to check out. Maura liked the woman with her bright, dark eyes and deep, brown curls. She reminded Maura of a dolphin because she exuded happiness and joy. It was obvious she loved her store and the items she sold. She thought of an octopus and their garden of colorful shells and rocks lovingly collected to put in their den.

The owner introduced herself as Jazzlyn and said, "I saw you two admiring some of our gift items. We have a hallway with a gallery if you're looking for other gifts."

"Gallery?" Rory asked. He turned and saw a hallway filled with paintings. His eyes lit up. "Are you taking consignments?"

"Yes, as a matter of fact, I am."

Rory pulled out his phone and shared Maura's paintings with her.

"These are lovely! They would sell easily here. Are they framed?" she asked, along with several other questions.

Rory said he could get them framed in a few days. They discussed pricing and when he could bring six paintings to the store.

"Have you ever considered putting these designs on mugs, tote bags, or shirts?"

"No, we haven't gotten there yet. It's an interesting thought. I'll look into it." He didn't hesitate and asked, "And before we finalize our purchases, can you show us the turquoise sea glass ring?"

"Certainly! This is created by one of our local artisans. Her work is amazing. Much of her glass is from local beaches. Some of it is from Puerto Rico that she harvests herself."

Jazzlynn handed the ring carefully to Rory, who, in turn, placed it on Maura's finger. It fit perfectly – almost as if it was custom-made for Maura.

"We'll take it," Rory said firmly as he held Maura's hand.

"Oh, Rory!" Maura breathed, happy tears filling her eyes. "Thank you! I will think of you every time I look at it. The color reminds me of your eyes."

"Aww," Jazzlyn commented, her eyes brimmed with tears at the touching scene. She put her hand to her heart and wiped her eyes with the other.

But Maura didn't notice. She only had eyes for Rory and stared into his turquoise eyes in wonder at this man.

RORY

Rory reddened and smiled at Maura before handing over his credit card. He was pleased that Maura felt comfortable in the stores. Some of his anxiety was relieved. She loved the gallery, but he did not like the owner. He ended up being a pompous ass, and Rory was glad the owner of the bookstore was going to take six of Maura's paintings on consignment. He wasn't sure what to do next. He debated on the aquarium. It was a stone's throw away from where they were, but he wasn't sure how Maura would react to seeing seals confined in tanks. He would need to talk to her.

Rory knew of another gallery just north of where they were. He felt compelled to share Maura's paintings.

The next gallery was in an old white house. It housed various artisans, including woodworkers, jewelry makers, ceramicists, printmakers, and painters. He liked to watch Maura as she ogled and studied the art around her. After she was fully engaged in studying the paintings and other pieces, he questioned the proprietors about Maura's artwork.

They were interested. In this gallery, you needed to become a member for several hundred dollars to be considered to show your work. It was an interesting process, and essentially, the artist supported the gallery and rented space to show their works. It was a good process, but new to Rory.

After he spoke with the proprietors, Rory perused the artwork in the gallery. It was bright and quiet, and Rory became lost in the artwork and his thoughts. Maura wanted to stay human and not return to being a seal. She wanted to be with him. It was what he wanted, but she had so much to learn. Socially, thus far, it was fine. Rory hoped that Maura could find a sustainable living as a human. This was one step. They would need to tackle her illiteracy, too. That was vital.

He had been moving about the gallery opposite Maura when he accidentally bumped into her and had been thinking about everything Maura needed to survive in the human world—identification, reading, learning about money, managing a household, and possibly driving a car.

"Oh!" Maura responded to the bump.

Her eyes were shiny and filled with hope and wonder. He thought he could drown in her eyes. He loved her, lusted her, and wanted to protect her in every way. His emotions swelled. He put his arm around her, slightly shaking his head to release the worrisome thoughts.

"Do you like it here?"

"Oh, yes!" she breathed. "Oh, Rory! Look at this art! I would love to create something like this. I don't know what the paint is. I could try it in watercolor. I would need a lot more of it to create something large like this."

Rory looked at the paintings she indicated. They were large seascapes in oils. Some of them were huge.

"Oil paints are different from watercolors and acrylics. You would need large canvases, an easel, and lots of paint, brushes, and turpentine," Rory answered. "Why don't you watch a few videos on it when we get home – to see if you want to explore the medium? I will look into the supplies."

"Oh! I can only imagine what I could paint on a large canvas. And I could paint the underwater world. Do you think people would like that?" she asked.

"All of your paintings show your heart. It's something that makes them so attractive to view. Your heart and emotions come through what you create. They're incredible, Maura. You are incredible," Rory told her emotion, threatening him.

"Art should come from the heart. It's integral to a good piece," a voice said behind them, overhearing some of their conversation.

One proprietor approached them during their discussion. She was a tall woman with long blond hair caught in a pretty clip at the back, dressed in tailored black pants and an embroidered purple silk tunic. She looked extremely elegant.

"Are you Maura?" she asked.

Maura nodded, albeit a bit shyly.

"I'm Elizabeth Curran. Your work is lovely. I hope you will consider joining our gallery. I spoke to Rory about membership," she introduced herself. Elizabeth continued, "Where did you study art? Do you have a MFA?"

Maura looked baffled and a little uncomfortable.

Rory jumped in to save the conversation. "Maura is self-taught. She's only started drawing and painting recently."

"Really?" Elizabeth responded with interest. "You have an amazing talent. It would be best if you explored some different mediums. I love your graphite work and those designs!"

Maura blushed prettily, Rory thought. He knew she was nervous because she tucked a strand of her long black hair behind her tiny ears.

"Thank you. Those are renditions of my sand paintings," Maura admitted to Elizabeth.

"Excuse me, did you say sand paintings?" Elizabeth asked, puzzled.

Rory spoke up. "Sculptures made with natural materials, like Jon Foreman. I think some people call it 'land art.' They are eventually washed away by wind or water."

"Do you have photographs of your sculptures?" Elizabeth asked.

Maura shook her head. "No, they're more of a meditative process."

Elizabeth nodded knowingly. "The next time you create your 'sand paintings,' you should photograph them," she suggested. "They would make great cards or small pictures to sell."

Elizabeth and Jazzlynn's suggestions opened Rory's eyes to monetizing Maura's art. It would be something they need to look into, and likely, a website. His head swam a bit.

"Thank you, Elizabeth. You've been extremely helpful. Maura and I will be in touch about the membership in the next couple of weeks," Rory told her.

He shook her hand and gave her one of his business cards.

"You can contact Maura through my number. It's a long story, but she lost her phone," he lied.

"Thank you for coming in. It's been a pleasure meeting you," Elizabeth told them, and she reached out a hand for Maura to shake.

Maura glanced at Rory and awkwardly extended her hand. He would need to tell her about handshakes. They had a lot to discuss.

He took Maura's elbow gently and steered her out the door and back to the car.

"Lunch?" he suggested. "We have a lot to talk about."

Maura nodded. She seemed to be in a daze.

They got in the car. Rory fiddled with his phone looking for restaurants and trying to decide on which one. Maura remained quiet as he scrolled through his phone. Finally, he put the phone down and started to drive.

They drove past the aquarium, and Maura's head whipped around, seeing the seal on a huge sign.

"Look at that!" she cried. "What is that?"

Rory shifted in his seat as much as he could within the confines of the seatbelt. It took him a moment to answer. "That's an aquarium. People visit to view the marine animals in tanks. Some of them are trained to entertain. I thought about taking you there but didn't know how you would feel about it."

"Marine animals in tanks?" Maura asked faintly, turning pale.

"There's treated well, I think the aquarium has a good reputation. It's smaller than many across the United States."

"But, animals in tanks?" Maura asked again.

"Some of it's for education and research, to learn more about marine species," Rory defended. "And sometimes, if an animal is injured and can't return to the wild, they stay in aquariums, where they can live safely."

Maura craned around to look at the aquarium fading in the distance. She looked worried. Rory reached over to take her hand.

They drove silently for a few miles until Rory pulled into a small, crushed shell parking lot. He led her inside a lovely restaurant appointed with creamy walls and pillars and a crackling fireplace, its warmth spreading through the room. To Rory, it looked like an old colonial inn.

It was mid-afternoon, and there were few diners. The hostess led them to an intimate table on the far side of the bar and handed them menus. Rory looked them over quickly.

A waitress came over for their drink order. Rory ordered a dark beer and automatically asked what Maura would like. She looked perplexed, and he realized she had likely never ordered a drink, let alone been in a restaurant. He asked the waitress to give them a minute.

"Salty or sweet?" he asked her.

"Salty," she answered.

When the waitress returned, he asked for a Bloody Caesar for Maura and wondered belatedly how alcohol would affect a Selki. He tried not to worry about it; instead, he read the menu to Maura. She shrugged her shoulders and asked him to choose. So, Rory chose.

A few minutes later, the waitress returned with the drinks and various appetizers, from Oysters Rockefeller to a spicy crab cake and Insalata de Mare.

"This drink is something you drink slowly," Rory warned.

Maura nodded, sipped, and smiled. She liked the salty, savory drink, especially the shrimp and olives garnish. She dug into the appetizers, remarking on the variety of flavors. Rory was amused at her reaction to oysters on the half shell. Her eyes widened that they were so easy to eat and didn't have to break the shells.

"About your artwork," he broached, "Jazzlynn and Elizabeth had great ideas. It will take me a bit, but we can set up a website or hire someone to add your work to be purchased online. We can add your designs to things like cups, mugs, t-shirts, etc. It's costly, but I think you should become a member of Elizabeth's gallery. It will help get the word out about your artwork. I also liked her idea of photographing your sand paintings. Maybe you could make a couple this week, and I can take photos, preferably on a cloudier day."

Maura looked at him. "You know I don't understand much of this, right?"

He nodded. "I know. I'll explain everything as we go along. You'll be able to have some money to help you get along in the world. You'll be able to be independent."

Maura still looked at him, not understanding.

He sighed. "Don't worry. I'll help you through everything. If you intend to remain human, you need to find a way to live here."

The waitress returned with their lunches and asked if they wanted more drinks. Rory looked at Maura and asked how she was feeling. When she replied, 'Fine,' he ordered a second Bloody Caesar for her.

When they finished their meal and stood up to go, Maura swayed.

"What's wrong with me? I feel like I could tip over," she asked Rory, concerned.

He tried not to laugh and told Maura, "It's the alcohol. Sometimes, it sneaks up on you. And that's why they call it being 'tipsy,' because you feel like you'll tip over."

"I'm not sure I like it," Maura muttered, clutching Rory's arm.

"Are you all right?" he asked her once they were ensconced in the car.

"I think so. It took me by surprise," Maura admitted. "I've never had alcohol before."

"I should have told you only to have one drink. I'm sorry," Rory apologized.

"I'm feeling so, so," she hesitated and said, "loose, I think. The insides of my body feel like liquid." She giggled.

"Let's get you home," Rory suggested.

Maura nodded.

He told her to take great breaths of the salty air, and she instantly felt better. They got home and took Skipper outside. Rory wanted to look at her drawings and paintings again and pull the ones for the bookshop. Maura sat on the couch in the drawing room, watching him intently.

Her gaze pulled him away from studying the artwork. He looked at her quizzically and asked, "What?"

"I like watching you," she answered. "I like how you concentrate on things." She put her hand on his leg and looked into his eyes, pulling his concentration further from the artwork

"Rory, you are always pleasuring me. What can I do to pleasure you?" she asked.

His eyes grew wide, and then he had a somewhat mischievous grin. He unzipped his pants.

"For starters, you can kiss me here," and he pointed to the top of his penis.

She did, and he groaned.

"Don't stop," he told her, "Pretend it's me, devouring your nipples."

Maura looked up in surprise. "Really?" she asked.

Rory nodded, becoming stiffer with the anticipation of her lips wrapped around his penis.

Maura lowered her head and gave a kiss, and then two, and then a lick, and with Rory beginning to moan in pleasure, she took his thick shaft in her mouth. He clutched her hair.

"More," he asked in a ragged whisper, "please don't stop."

Maura continued to lick and nibble and suck on him. It was driving him crazy. He didn't want her to stop, but he wanted to be buried deep inside of her.

He sat up awkwardly, and his voice rasped, "Let's go to bed."

They lost their clothes as they went down the hallway. Rory buried himself inside Maura with a groan. She felt so damn good. He lost himself in her and thrust over and over until he climaxed, screaming her name.

23

MAURA

Maura lay awake long after Rory fell asleep. He had thrown a protective arm and leg over her and she snuggled in closer.

This man, she thought, and then Skipper pressed against her and put his head on her leg. This *man and his dog love me. And they saved me. But what's even more amazing is that this man wants me to successfully learn to be human and to live and thrive in this world. He believes in me. He believes in my art and thinks I can thrive as an artist and as a human being. I need to start believing in myself.*

Today had been an incredible day for her. Experiencing the extensive range of artistic styles at the gallery, Maura's brain flashed with the images of the art. She also had flashes of things she wanted to draw and paint in the future. Rory had opened up an entire new world – no, an entire new universe—to her.

She thought about his comment about remaining human and her need for independence. Right now, she was dependent on him for everything. And, although the break from pure survival from day to day was nice, it wasn't Maura. She was independent and had been all of her life. Rory was supportive and urged her to be independent again, which was nice. Remaining human. Is that something she wanted to do? Could she be successful as a human? She had so much to learn. It was overwhelming to begin to think about. But she had her art, and her art had part of her heart. She now knew the other part of her heart was with Rory. And she didn't know how to explain this to him. It was foreign to her seal way of life. She knew she had to communicate it to him, other than mating. She wanted him to know how important he was to her and how she appreciated his love and caretaking. She would need to think about this.

The different mediums intrigued Maura. Her hands itched to begin painting. Rory promised to share videos on oil painting techniques. And she wished, for the hundredth time, that she could read. She was sure there would be books on painting. The bookstore had a wide variety of books. Rory mentioned a library, but she didn't know what that was.

Maura patted Skipper and gently pushed him off the bed. She crept out and replaced her form with a pillow. Rory moaned but didn't wake. He was sleeping deeply because he was snoring lightly. Maura looked at him. He looked so innocent with his dark lashes long on his cheeks. She gave Skipper the 'stay' signal. He snuggled into Rory as if he knew her thoughts.

Maura went to the drawing room and looked at the supplies. Rory had picked up a couple of canvases. She had large tubes of paint that he had purchased. What could she use as a palette? And larger brushes? She remembered things in the kitchen that might work. Rory had used what he called a 'cookie sheet.' It was long, shallow, and flat. It would work perfectly if she could find it.

Maura went downstairs. She poked and prodded into the cupboards' recesses. Then she looked in drawers and found tin foil, plastic wrap, waxed paper, and parchment. She felt them between her fingers and put foil down first, followed by the waxed paper.

She returned to the drawing room, squeezed color onto the covered cookie sheet, grabbed her largest brush, and stared at the canvas. What should she paint? Images slid through her head. She took a deep breath and plunged in, painting swiftly and surely, creating a sky and clouds and then waves upon the water. In quick, rough strokes, an ocean scape appeared before her eyes. It reminded her of the large oils she had seen earlier that day. Far out in the water, she put the fin of a dolphin and the bobbing head of a seal. You wouldn't be able to see them unless you really looked. It was her secret, and she smiled at this.

The acrylics, she found, dried almost as fast as the watercolors. She needed to work fast to keep the painting going. At last, she was satisfied with the result and left the painting to dry on the desk completely. There was another canvas Rory had purchased, but Maura would think about what she wanted to paint. She returned to bed and climbed in carefully between her two men and dreamed of paintings to create.

Skipper tried to wake Maura the next morning. She moaned and batted him away.

"Are you all right?" she heard Rory's voice through a sleepy haze. Maura nodded.

"Painted," she mumbled.

"Ahh," was Rory's response.

"Come on, Skipper, leave Maura alone," Rory called to the dog.

Maura returned to dreamland, waking an hour later to find a steaming cup of coffee beside the bed. Rory climbed in beside her, sipping his hot, black coffee. Maura found she liked the bitter brew tempered with cinnamon, milk, and sugar.

"I saw your painting," he told Maura as he sipped. "I like it."

Maura blushed a little and reached for her coffee.

"I just had to experiment a little," she admitted.

"It's a little like the one we saw at the gallery, but different," Rory said.

"Did you find the secret?" Maura asked slyly.

"What?"

"You'll have to look carefully," she said she teased.

"Okay, challenge accepted."

They sipped their coffee. Maura leaned against Rory, and Skipper leaned against Maura.

"I love this," she admitted. "It reminds me of seals gathering on the beach, but better. It's comforting."

"I'm glad," Rory admitted. "Is the call of the sea still so strong?"

"I'm pretty happy as a human, but mostly because of you and Skipper. You two saved me. I was thinking a lot about that last night. I'm not sure that would happen in the seal world. We're on our own a lot. We get together for mating and haul out to rest. But, usually, we're on our own. The Selki are more familial, and I miss my family."

"We're family now," Rory said, putting down his coffee and scooting closer to her, putting his head in her lap.

"I'm glad. I wish I could find my sister, Kelsi. Some of the herd said she was in New Jersey living with a human. My sister Rhona," Maura paused and shuddered, closing her eyes, "I don't know if she is alive or dead."

"We might be able to find Kelsi," Rory said, "I don't know how right now, but I'll think about it."

"Really? Is that possible?"

"There are so many ways to track humans now," Rory began.

Maura interrupted, "She's not human! You said so yourself that I needed all kinds of human identification. Kelsi would too."

"I hope the man she is with loves her and will help her with those things, just like I want to help you to stay in the human world. If you want to, that is," he broke off, and a question lay in his eyes.

She stroked his curly dark hair. He closed his eyes as if he was Skipper. Maura couldn't imagine being any happier than she was at this moment. Their energies filled one another and coalesced. It was near to their lovemaking but almost better. She closed her eyes and wished for many mornings like this.

"I do want to be with you," Maura reassured him. "I am so happy being with you and Skipper. I feel I am truly myself with you, especially when creating my art. You do need to understand that I still long for many freedoms of swimming in the wild sea. There's nothing like torpedoing through the water, exploring kelp forests, and the joy of being in the water. Be patient with me."

He held her close. "I'll be patient," he told her, "But you may need to remind me sometimes."

"I can do that," Maura assured Rory, reaching up to cup his cheek, leaning over, and giving him a long, lingering kiss.

24

RORY

They stayed like that for a long while, his head in her lap and Maura stroking his hair. She put her coffee on the bedside table. Rory turned and kissed her stomach, relishing the taste of her skin before stretching up next to her and putting his arm and leg over her again. And then, he moved on top of her, entering her in small increments. Maura moaned and squirmed, wanting him completely inside of her. But Rory wanted to take things slowly, and he told her so. He touched her slowly, sensuously, running his finger and then his hand over her body, touching every inch of her skin that he could reach. And when he was fully inside of her, he moved in small ways to feel her muscles hug his penis, clenching and unclenching as if it were something alien that pulled him more inside of her, feeling the velvety inside skin of her vagina like a silken bed of pleasure. At one point, he stopped moving and told Maura to be still. They lay completely intertwined and joined together, not even speaking, just feeling. They lay like this for a few minutes, and then Rory moved in infinitesimal amounts and brought them to a quiet roar of passion.

Afterward, he held her, letting the day march on, not caring about time or anything but holding Maura. That is until his phone rang.

Rory groaned and reached for his phone. He answered and listened, leaning on one elbow and covering his face with one hand.

"Okay, okay. I'll be there as soon as I can," Rory said to the faceless voice.

He ended his call. Shock and disbelief enveloped him. He seemed to stare at nothing.

He felt Maura's hand on him, and her eyes held questions. He gulped in a great breath of air. Words refused to come at first. He felt himself grow cold and begin to shake.

"Rory! Rory! What's wrong?" Maura's frightened voice inched into his daze.

"The project I was working on, the place caught on fire. The whole thing is in ruins," he stated flatly.

"Oh, no!" Maura answered.

"I need to go," he said, throwing on jeans and a sweatshirt. "I don't know when I'll be back. You'll be all right?" he asked lamely. "I'm now remembering I have no way to reach you. You have no phone. I don't have a landline anymore. Maura, I..." He broke off and shook his head helplessly.

"I'll be fine," Maura assured him. "I have Skipper here. I'll work on more drawings."

Rory wanted to say, "I love you." It was on the tip of his tongue, but he wasn't sure yet. He felt it inside. He felt it in every part of his being with Maura, but he couldn't tell her...not yet.

"I'll be back as soon as I can," he promised, quickly kissing her.

As he drove, he wondered why he had not said "I love you" to Maura. Would she know? After all, she was a seal and didn't know many human ways. Would she care? He bought her the sea glass ring. Didn't that mean something? Did she know the significance of a ring? Probably not. She was innocent in so many ways.

She had no phone. He would need to rectify that and teach her how to use it. There were so many things he had to teach her. In many ways, she was his Pygmalion. He didn't feel that way about her. He didn't feel he was molding her to be his perfect woman. He accepted her from day one from finding her on the beach. He didn't understand where his feelings for her came from. They were just there. It was like breathing for him. Maura was part of him and his every breath. And he wanted her to stay human. He wanted her to be with him forever. And to live in the human world successfully, she needed to learn how to be human. He wished he had someone to talk with about this and a woman to whom she could look up. His mom's face skittered through his brain, as well as Lizzie's. They were two of the best women he knew, but he could imagine their disbelief that Maura was a Selki.

But he hadn't told Maura this and wondered if that was a problem. Right now, he had bigger problems to attend to, and he had to trust the universe that everything would turn out all right in the end.

He drove mindlessly to the job site, worried at what he would find at the job site. John, the foreman, had called, and his voice was ragged with worry, anger, and frustration. John was one of the calmest people he knew, and the tone of his voice put Rory on edge.

The closer he came to the job site, black smoke poured into the sky, and vehicles with flashing lights appeared in the distance. He had to park back from the building and pulled over on the side of the road. The air was acrid and full of smoke. He coughed and pulled his shirt over his nose. Rory's heart sank. The beautiful building he had designed was now charred and in ruins. It was a skeleton of its former self the metal beam slumped like anorexic scarecrows blackened by the fire

He saw the foreman, his face grave. What could have caused this? Faulty wiring? That was the only thing that made sense. He got out of his car to speak with John for updated news.

"John!" he cried, trying to be heard over the noise of the emergency equipment.

John hadn't heard him. John was in as much shock as he. He stared disbelievingly at the charred remains of the project. Rory touched his elbow and said his name again, and John whirled around.

"Rory!" he replied, obviously relieved to see a familiar face. "This is crazy unbelievable."

Rory tugged at his hair in a frustrated gesture. "I know. Who can we talk to?"

John nodded at the one fireman leaning against a car emblazoned with "Fire Chief."

"Him, I guess."

They walked over and introduced themselves. The man was polite and introduced himself as Doug.

"What happened, Doug?" Rory pressed.

"No word yet," Doug commented, "this is an ongoing investigation. It was a new structure, right?"

Both Rory and John nodded.

"This is an investigation now. We'll investigate the scene and take samples to the lab to determine the cause of the fire. This isn't something that can be solved off the cuff or in an hour like they do on television," Doug warned. "It's a lot of documentation, collecting evidence, interviews, and gathering testimonies."

"I understand. Please let us know if there's anything we can do to assist. I have the blueprints if you need them," Rory offered. "Here's my card. Call me when you can."

Doug nodded, thanking him and tucking Rory's card into a pocket, but had his eyes returned to the scene ahead of him.

They turned to go. Rory walked John back to his car, his mouth dry. He tried to start a conversation but instead began to cough with the smoke. John slapped him on his back, and Rory cleared his throat.

"Any ideas what caused this?" Rory rasped.

John shook his head. "Dunno. I can't think of anything. I thought we were careful. Who's to gain from something like this if it was foul play?"

Rory shook his head in response, "I guess we'll have to wait for a report."

25

MAURA

Maura lay still after Rory left. Skipper jumped up and lay pressed against her side. They both missed Rory's presence. She patted his head and let herself sink into a doze. She thought of Rory rushing off to his project, wherever it was, and the possible fire. She wished she was with him, but that wasn't a good idea. Not now. She thought she would be in the way with her ignorance of human things.

She dozed for another hour with Skipper before getting up to make them both scrambled eggs. Afterward, she dressed and took Skipper for a long walk on the beach. It was a fine December day with bright sunshine. Seagulls wheeled overhead, and the ocean was quiet, with gentle breakers coming to shore. She stared at the deep blue water for several minutes before searching for shells and rocks to create a sand painting.

As promised, she made a design near the steps to Rory's house, using a moon snail shell at the center and oyster shells and seaweed radiating outwards in a complex mandala. Small slipper shells added detail.

Even with the sunshine, the air had a wintry bite. Maura was chilled through by the time she was finished. Skipper was leaning on her for warmth as well.

"Okay, Skipper. Let's hope Rory gets home before this washes away," she told the dog. "Brr. I'm cold! This is when I miss my pelt."

Maura rubbed her arms and ran up the steps to the house. She felt chilled to the bone, but she wasn't sure how to make coffee, and she wasn't sure she wanted more. Soup sounded good. Rory had taught her how to use the microwave, so surely it was easy to make.

Maura took a can of soup from the cupboard. She looked at the ring on top to open it. It couldn't be that hard to open. She pulled, but nothing happened. She used her other hand to hold the can in place, and when she pulled, her finger was in the way of the lid, and it made a neat slice in her thumb.

At first, she didn't know she was cut until she saw the blood welling from the wound. And then, the pain hit – a stinging, stabbing pain that made her thumb throb. Fear paralyzed her. She wasn't sure what to do at first. She could only stare at the blood – her blood, coming from the wound, dripping on the counter, leaving dark red splotches Maura felt a little faint. She had never seen her own blood before, not as a seal or human. It made sense to stop the blood, and she grabbed a kitchen towel and wrapped it around her thumb. It hurt.

She sat, holding her injured thumb, wondering what to do. She was grateful she wasn't in the ocean because blood drew sharks. Maura shuddered. She hated sharks. She had lost friends due to shark bites and attacks. She remembered Ronan, one of her family's friends. He was a fine, young seal who had been sweet on Rhona, and after he died, she seemed lost. And, now, she was missing. No one knew where Rhona went when the virus hit. She was ill with the virus, too, and drifted away from the herd. Maura didn't know if she was alive or dead. And then there was Nami, another Selki. She was adventurous and loved to swim in the moonlight as a seal and in her human form. A Great White Shark snatched her from them near Cape Cod. It was so fast. She was there one minute and gone the next on a starry night with the full moon. The other Selki had been dancing on the beach. Nami was in seal form, reveling in the waves when it happened. Maura remembered the shock of watching their friend perish in the jaws of the shark. The dancing ceased and they huddled together, holding one another, mourning the loss of Nami. Maura still mourned the loss of her friend who seemed to always have stars in her eyes and great ambition. She was a Selki who would understand why she was still in human form. Maura wished she could talk with her. Maura shuddered, hating sharks. They were vicious. She didn't like their cold, dead eyes, and she always avoided them at all costs.

Skipper was worried about her and hovered nearby, sniffing her thumb wrapped in the towel.

"I think I'm okay, Skipper," she told him. "Just a little dizzy. Let's go to the couch."

Maura made her way to the living room and lay on the couch. Skipper jumped up and put his head on her legs. She closed her eyes.

She heard the door, and Rory was home. Skipper barked, alerting him to where they were, but he didn't move off her.

Rory's eyes widened when he saw her on the couch with the towel around her hand.

"What happened?" he asked, concern filling his voice as he rushed to Maura.

"I was being stupid. I was cold and hungry and wanted to make soup. I didn't open the can very well." She held up the hand for him to see.

Gently, Rory unwrapped the towel and saw the blood.

"Ouch," he commented. "Let's get this cleaned up and bandaged."

He led her to the bathroom, where he cleaned and bandaged the hurt thumb with gauze and tape. Afterward, he patted her arm soothingly and said, "It's almost all better now."

Rory led her back to the couch.

"Still cold?" he asked.

"A little," she admitted.

Rory dropped the soft throw from the back of the couch and tucked it around her shoulders.

"I'll go and make us some soup," he said.

"I should be taking care of you!" Maura protested. "You've had a horrible morning, I'm sure!"

"It's fine," he said. "No worries," he exited the living room and returned to the kitchen to make the soup.

Skipper stayed with Maura. She shook her head in amazement.

"He's amazing, isn't he?" she told Skipper.

He looked at her with those large eyes, and she knew he understood.

2 6

RORY

When Rory got home, he expected to find Maura drawing and painting. He was shocked to see her pale and wan on the couch with a towel around her hand. It was disturbing to find her hurt, and he realized for the millionth time that she wasn't a human and didn't know the human world—even though anyone could cut themselves on a can. She didn't know about bandages and Band-Aids.

Her lack of knowledge about the human world worried him. She was all right, for the most part, around the house. He had been teaching her many basic skills, but sometimes, the realization of her lack of human knowledge and life was overwhelming.

He worked on making the soup and took in two steaming soup mugs and their favorite saltine crackers with butter on a tray. Maura smiled up at him.

"Thank you."

"No problem," he returned.

They ate their lunch. With a little food, Maura began to get her color back.

"What happened at the job site?" she asked.

Rory's face crumbled. His eyes were filled with worry, a touch of fear, and some anger. "We lost most of the building. It's completely gutted and a burned-out shell of a building. It burned completely, and nothing is salvageable. They need to investigate what happened. The remainder of the property has a lot of smoke damage. I don't know if it's a total loss or what."

"I'm so sorry. Is there anything I can do?"

"Just be here. Please." His eyes pleaded with her.

She smiled prettily. "I can do that." Changing the subject, she said, "I made a sand painting at the bottom of the stairs. I'm not sure about the tide and if it's still there. We could go and look. This was practice because I haven't made one in a long time."

"Cool," Rory said. "Let me get my camera, and we can check it out."

When they reached the bottom of the stairs, the tide was rising rapidly. Rory got a few shots of the sand painting with the foamy sea water coming right up to the edge of it. He showed Maura the photos on the screen of his digital camera, shading it for her to see.

"It's a beautiful sand painting, Maura. I'll email these photos to Elizabeth and see if she was referring to something like this," Rory told Maura and suggested, "If the weather is good next weekend, maybe you can make some more?"

He glanced at Maura. Her face was blank. He realized she knew nothing about photographs, emailing, and using phones and computers. He sighed a little. Once more thing—more things to put on the list of things to teach her.

Back at the house, Rory uploaded the photos and emailed them to Elizabeth, modeling and discussing what he was doing to explain the process to Maura. He fished around in his desk and found an old greeting card to explain how Elizabeth thought they could put photographs of her sand paintings on cards to sell.

He was interrupted by a ringing phone. Glancing at the screen, he saw it was his mom's call. He answered, glancing guiltily at Maura, and said, 'Hello.'

"Rory!" his mother's voice rang clearly through the phone. "How are you? Where are you? Have you dropped off the face of the earth? I haven't talked to you in weeks. Lizzie called me. She said you were in a new relationship. How is it going? What are your plans for the holidays?" She said all this in a rush, not permitting Rory to interrupt.

"Slow down, mom. I'm doing mostly fine. Yes, I met someone. You'll love her. I haven't thought about the holidays, and the current project I'm working on has been a nightmare. I've been involved with it today. It caught fire."

There was a gasp on the other end of the phone. His mom asked for details, and Rory shared what had happened that morning and that he had just returned from the job site.

"Look, Mom, I'm tired and smoky from the fire. I'm sorry I haven't been in touch, but it's been a whirlwind."

"So, tell me more about this girl, Rory," his mom pressed.

"Maura? She's lovely, mom. She's an artist. Her work will be featured in a couple of galleries nearby."

Rory stood and went out to the kitchen to talk more privately. Thinking better of it, he stepped outside.

"Mom, I think she's 'the one,'" he admitted.

"That's pretty serious, son. I would love to meet this woman."

Rory answered, "I'd like to bring Maura to the city. She's never been to New York. Let's plan on getting together in a couple of weeks, okay? Love you, Mom."

He went back inside to find Maura patiently waiting during his phone call.

"My mom," he explained, "she was checking in because I haven't talked with her in a couple of weeks. She would like us to come for a visit. She lives in the city."

Maura nodded. He continued, "How do you feel about that?"

"To be honest, terrified," Maura admitted. "But I do want to meet your mom. I'm a little worried about what she'll think of me."

"I think you will like her. I think she will love you. I am a little pissed at Lizzie for tattling about you."

Maura gave a little shrug at this, "Perhaps Lizzie thought she was doing you a favor. She's worried for you."

"I guess so. I need to talk to her."

"Will you tell your mom and Lizzie I am a Selki?"

Rory tugged at his hair before he answered, "Well, that is the elephant in the room," he said with emphasis. And looking up and seeing Maura's blank stare, he chuckled, "Sorry, human expression. It's a way of stating something obvious and uncomfortable. I have been wracking my brain on how and when to break the news to them. It's not going to be an easy conversation, and I don't know if they will believe me – or us."

Maura went over to Rory, and he opened his arms. She entered his protective circle, and they held each other.

"I don't have any wisdom to give you," Maura said, her face pressed against him. "The truth always seems to be the best thing."

He nodded, his face pressed into her hair.

"I know. We'll figure it out," he said wearily, "but right now, I need to get to the store to get frames for the pictures for Jazzlyn." And he brightened, "And you'll love this store. It is full of art supplies." His mood changed, and he grinned at her a little mischievously. "I can hardly wait to see what you think."

2 7

MAURA

The arts and crafts store's bright, white fluorescent lights almost blinded Maura. The glaring light bounced off the bright white metal shelves. It was full to the brim of things Maura had never seen before. Rory grabbed a shopping cart and wheeled it to the aisle of painting supplies. At the aisle's entrance, she could see stacks of canvases, paints, and pads of varieties of paper. She was stunned at the abundance of art materials. She thought she had entered an art paradise. She couldn't move.

Rory was smirking. "Like?"

"Oh, Rory!" she whispered in awe. "This is an amazing place!"

His tone became more serious. "If you want to work in oils and acrylics on large canvases, you'll need to get an easel."

On his way down the aisle, he picked up one of the largest canvases and demonstrated how it worked on a floor model. Maura gasped. This was exactly what she wanted, and she nodded vigorously.

"Yes, oh yes!" she cried. "That would be perfect."

Rory nodded. "I thought so. You were taken with the large canvases at the gallery."

He picked up a large box and put it in the cart.

"Why don't you choose three or four canvases you like?" he suggested.

"And you'll need paints and brushes," he advised, pointing to the other side of the aisle where the supplies were neatly stacked.

As if in a dream, Maura chose three huge canvases. She envisioned the seascapes she would paint—a calm, blue sea, the sea in a storm, and perhaps a painting under the sea. With paints, she chose large tubs and tubes of acrylics since she had not worked with oils yet. She knew she would need larger brushes, so she looked over the selection, fingering soft and stiffer bristles. She could hardly wait to get home to begin painting.

Maura was stunned by the variety of supplies and art on display as they walked to the back of the store for the frames. Several crafts looked interesting. Maybe someday, but she felt she could spend her lifetime exploring painting.

Rory mentioned purchasing pre-made frames, and he led her to that aisle. They chose simple, black metal frames to showcase her artwork.

Darkness was gathering when they left the store, and the cold air nipped at them. Maura's eyes stung with the cold. She leaned as close as she could to Rory, but he pushed the heavy cart with the supplies vigorously ahead. She drifted from him by a few steps, moving slightly more slowly, and looked up. Between the bright lights of the parking lot and the clouds, she couldn't see the stars tonight. That was something she missed as a seal. Even though she didn't like to swim at night, the beauty of the starry sky from the remote places where she hauled out was dazzling. The stars were always brilliant, and the constellations were constant friends from wherever she was on the Atlantic seaboard. She wasn't sure she liked the artificial lights in the parking lot. Rory called to her, and she woke out of her thoughts and climbed into the seat beside him, craning around to see the new art supplies lodged in the rear of the car. Rory suggested they pick up sushi for dinner. She remembered Rory said she would like it earlier. Rory pointed out the holiday lights and explained that people were enthusiastic about holiday décor. Maura was enchanted with the lights and decorations, especially the white and blue lights. She laughed, pointed at some of the air-filled decorations, and saw bushes and trees outlined in lights. It was magical.

He drove to a small strip mall and asked her to stay in the car while he ran in to get the order. She watched him go into the night and enter a small establishment. Moments later, he came out with a large paper bag. He asked her to hold onto it in the car. Maura smelled fish, and also a piquant smell of something interesting. Her stomach growled in anticipation.

When they got home, Rory sat a large cardboard box on the kitchen table. Inside were smaller boxes containing interesting-looking rolls of food, fish eggs of varying sizes, and slices of raw fish on top of a nugget of something. Her mouth watered in anticipation.

Rory pulled out sticks from a drawer, explained they were chopsticks, and modeled how to use them. She found this difficult until he told her to hold one like a pencil she drew and showed her how to support the other. She practiced picking up food. She was successful several times but resorted to picking up the food with her fingers.

The sushi was so delicious. The fish was fresh and tender.

She stared at Rory in wonder.

"What?" he questioned.

"You," Maura said, " are a most amazing human. You care so much. I don't know what to do for you in return."

Rory looked embarrassed. "Maura, thank you for the compliments. I'm just being me. There's nothing special. As for humans, not all of them are nice."

"Oh, I know," she interrupted and visibly shuddered. "Bad humans clubbed my baby brother for his pelt."

"What?" Rory cried aghast. "Oh, Maura, oh my God! I'm so sorry. Losing someone close to you is bad enough, but like that..." he broke off and shook his head. He put his hand over hers and squeezed. "I've heard about humans doing that, but I thought the practice was banned long ago."

"It still happens," Maura said darkly, "when the seal pups are resting, and the moms are going out to find food. The men come and club the babies over and over. It's sickening. They even check to see if the baby seal is still alive, and if not, continue to bash in their heads."

Rory winced, "That's horrible. I'm sorry. They don't believe in the sacredness of life."

"That's why I am glad you are you, and you found and helped me." She looked into his eyes, "I was raised on stories that men were very bad to Selki women. They would rape them and keep them prisoner, keeping their pelts hidden for years. Usually, in the end, they found their pelts and returned to the sea. But those bad men were always in the nightmares of my sisters and me. I appreciate you for being you –being good and kind. And the fact that you don't want to keep me prisoner is all the more reason why I want to stay with you. You have opened the world to me."

Rory blushed over her words. He was at a loss about what to say but answered, "You're welcome. I'm tired, but I want to get this easel together tonight. Will you help me get the stuff from the car?"

"Of course."

They took Skipper outside before hauling the things from the car to the drawing room. Rory went to his little shed to get tools to assemble the easel. Maura set up her paints and brushes in anticipation. She leaned the canvases against the wall and watched Rory put together the easel. He seemed frustrated, crumpling up the directions and throwing them across the room, but he was dogged about finishing the job, sorting through the hardware, and turning the pieces of wood this way and that way. Finally, it was together, and with Maura's help, he stood it up next to the desk and put a canvas in place.

Maura jumped and clapped her hands. "Oh, Rory! It's amazing!"

She hugged him and kissed him on the cheek, but when she did, he turned and kissed her on the mouth. Her stomach fluttered, and the heat traveled south. His kisses deepened, and so did hers. He wanted to mate, she thought. And, in a bold move, she took his hand and slid it under her shirt so that he could touch her breast.

Rory snapped the fingers of his other hand and pointed to Skipper to get off the couch. Offended, the dog grunted and moved to the floor while Rory guided Maura to the chaise lounge section of the couch, where they could stretch out almost fully. Maura put a pillow underneath her bottom and pulled up her knees to allow him deeper access. She pulled him towards her, wanting him to bury himself inside of her. Maura was pleased to hear Rory moan with pleasure. She moaned with each thrust, too, as they sent electric tingles throughout her body. They climaxed quickly and lay panting in each other's arms for several minutes.

Rory buried his face in her breasts, "Oh, Maura, I can't get enough of you," he moaned.

"I feel exactly the same," she told him. "Exactly."

She could feel him smile against her skin, and she closed her eyes, feeling like the luckiest Selki in existence.

2 8

RORY

Rory needed to tell Maura he loved her, but something held him back, and he wasn't sure what that was. Was it due to her being a Selki? He didn't think he had issues with that, but maybe, deep down, he did. Her presence was life-changing. Her need for him was a heady mix of blessing and burden.

They had moved to the bed, and he held her tightly as if she were a precious jewel to hold and protect. She was sleeping deeply, but he was awake and overtired. He wished he could sleep, and his thoughts kept tumbling around in his head.

Their conversation earlier had been interesting. She said seals do not care or love like humans, and many Selkis felt the same. Were they incapable of love? Would she scoff at him or leave if he professed to be in love with her? He wondered who he could talk to about this.

As if the Universe was in sync with his thoughts, Rory's phone rang. He answered quickly so as not to disturb Maura. It was Lizzie asking to meet for coffee tomorrow morning. Just him. He agreed.

Maura looked at him drowsily, roused by the sound of his voice. She looked at him quizzically.

"It was Lizzie. She wants to talk to me. I'm going to meet her for coffee tomorrow," he explained.

"I don't think she likes me," Maura said as she yawned, waking a little. "What gave you that idea?"

Maura shrugged, "Just a feeling. She's worried about you. She's afraid, I think."

"Afraid?"

"That I might get in the way of your friendship. She loves you, you know."

"Yeah, like a sister," Rory insisted.

"Exactly. That's a tight bond. We can't let that happen. I haven't been around her much to assure her. It's uncomfortable, so please tell her I'm not threatening your friendship."

He met Lizzie at their favorite coffee house in town. As per usual, he was early, and Lizzie was late.

"Sorry, bro," she greeted him, hugging him. "How the heck are you?"

"Get your coffee, Lizzie," Rory suggested, "and then we can talk."

"Uh, oh, sounds serious," she teased.

Lizzie went to get her coffee and sat across from him.

"How are things?" she asked.

"Fine," he returned. "Actually, pretty good," and he grinned.

"I'm still sensing a 'but' in there," she pushed.

Rory took a sip of his coffee before answering.

"It's Maura. She's 'the one.' I know it. I'm just having trouble with the 'L' word," he confessed, "and I don't know what's holding me back. She's amazing, and in this short relationship we've had, I can't imagine living without her."

"Wow," Lizzie said, "I didn't expect that. But, if you're having trouble with the "L" word, shouldn't that set of alarm bells? My gut feeling is that there's 'something' about her," Lizzie paused and made finger quotes before continuing, "that I can't put my finger on. How did you meet again?"

Rory told Lizzie about Maura looking for her sister, losing her stuff to some bad guys, and getting sick. Lizzie didn't believe him and told him so.

"That's a bunch of bullshit!" Lizzie's voice was raised.

The quiet conversation of the diners was momentarily stilled. People stared. The whoosh of the expresso machine sounded loud in the silence. Lizzie flushed.

"It's all right, folks," she announced, "No harm, no foul. Go back to your coffees."

It took a moment, and Lizzie stared down some people, but eventually, they all returned to their coffees and conversations. She turned to Rory and whispered vehemently, "You've never lied to me that I know of, but this doesn't seem quite right. Is that what *she* sold you? And you believed it? You're a softy, Rory. You have such a big heart. I don't want to see anyone take advantage of you. You say you love her. Do you think she loves you back? I'm telling you, there's something weird with her, but I can't quite get a handle on it. You know my grandmother had the 'sight.' I may have a little too," she confided. "But something isn't sitting right with me about Maura. And I'm worried about you."

Rory sat, took more sips of his coffee, and wrestled with telling Lizzie the truth. Would she believe him? He looked at her. She looked back and raised an eyebrow.

"Did you meet her online? She could be a whack-a-doodle, Rory. She didn't seem like it, but you never know. She could be a whack-a-doodle. There's something...," and she trailed off.

Rory barked a laugh that turned into a laughing fit with tears streaming down his face. He got himself under control as Lizzie was glaring at him.

"She's not a whack-a-doodle, Lizzie," he said, "but there is something. I don't know if I can tell you or not. I don't know if you'll believe me."

"Let me guess, she's under witness protection?"

Rory shook his head.

"Well, I don't know!" Lizzie cried, frustrated and slamming her cup down. "I'm grasping at straws here, Rory."

People turned their heads again. Rory looked down at his coffee, bemused by Lizzie.

"Then *tell* me," Lizzie commanded.

Rory took a deep breath. How could he explain Maura? How would Lizzie ever believe she was a Selki? What did his mom always say —start talking. She would tell him he would build a story, one brick at a time, and that it would all come together in the end.

"Maura," he began and stopped to take a sip.

He stared into his coffee for a full minute. When he looked up, Lizzie looked like she would explode if he didn't start talking. He looked her straight in the eye.

"Lizzie, Maura isn't like us."

"What do you mean? Is she an alien?" Lizzie asked, trying to temper humor into their conversation.

Rory seriously answered, "No, not quite. But you're sort of on the right track."

Lizzie's eyes goggled.

"She's a Selki."

"A what? What's that?" Lizzie asked. "Is that a foreign country I don't know about? Is it a weird religious cult? Tell me Rory."

"It's a person who's a seal in the water and a person on land. You might have seen a movie or read about a Selki in folklore. I couldn't believe it. I found her on the beach, and she was really, really sick. She had her sealskin draped over her."

"Don't you think it was some kind of weird cosplay?" Lizzie asked skeptically.

"That's what I thought at first, too. I thought she was a wild swimmer who really got into her role and dressed up as a seal. I thought it was really weird, too. But once she felt better, she explained what she was."

"And you believed her?" Lizzie interrupted.

"She showed me, Lizzie. She put on her sealskin, and it magically formed around her. She went for a swim in it. And then, I saw her come and peel it off like a costume. I thought I was seeing things or going nuts or something, but it's true!"

Lizzie looked at him. "I wish I had something stronger than coffee right now. Bro, this is weird stuff. If it were anyone else, I wouldn't believe them, but it's you. So that's why you came up with that cock and bull story about her looking for her sister and her stuff being stolen?"

Rory nodded miserably. "She has no identification. I don't know how she's going to make it in the human world. Lizzie, I have to teach her *everything*. You have no idea."

"Is it worth it?" Lizzie asked, "That she's sort of your Pygmalion?"

Rory started at this. He had only entertained the thought of Pygmalion briefly.

"I guess I would have to do some soul-searching on that one," he said quietly, "but I love her, Lizzie – like I've never loved anyone else. I don't want to live without her."

"Well, you've certainly been bitten by the love bug. But you do seem tortured. Teaching her how to be human is a huge commitment. Are you ready for that? This isn't someone you can break up with down the road. It's a lifetime commitment."

"I know, I know! I've been afraid to tell her I love her. For God's sake, Lizzie, she's part seal! Human emotions are only part of her world. I keep thinking she will laugh at me, take her pelt, and swim far away. I don't know if I could handle it."

"Why? What's the harm? Don't be a chicken-shit! You're afraid she'll go back to the ocean. You have to face it, Rory. That's a choice, but she has a pretty sweet life with you, whether she loves you or not."

"You're always the skeptic, aren't you?" Rory replied, a little fed up with Lizzie's sarcasm and doubt. He wanted support, not someone to shoot down his dream. "And she's not a user, despite what you think, Lizzie."

"Whoa, Rory. I'm not trying to hurt your feelings or tell you you're wrong for loving Maura. I guess I want to give you a shot of reality. I can't imagine having to teach her how to be human. How do you do it?"

"One day at a time. And Lizzie, she's an amazing artist. Her drawings and paintings have blown me away. It's like they've been bottled up inside her for years and are now just coming out. We set her up with some consignments, and she's been offered space in a gallery."

"Really?" Lizzie was amazed. "I'd like to see this art."

"Come over any time. Trust me, you'll be amazed."

"Okay, I will," Lizzie said. "But now I need to run. I'm going to be late for work."

"Thanks," Rory told her. "Thank you. I needed to tell someone. It's all been surreal. Fantastic, but surreal."

"I can only begin to imagine," Lizzie replied. "But hang in there and trust the F-ing Universe, okay, Bro?"

"Okay, Lizzie. Love you," Rory said as he hugged her goodbye.

As usual, Lizzie buoyed him up. She was a good friend.

29

MAURA

Maura was slightly surprised when Rory was apologetic as he left for coffee with Lizzie. She didn't mind, and she certainly wasn't jealous. She wanted to paint. It was all she could do to sit with him for a few minutes. She kept glancing longingly at the stairs when they were having coffee in the kitchen. He didn't seem to notice. He seemed preoccupied and lost in thought.

She scooted up the stairs with Skipper in tow as soon as he left. He settled onto the couch, and Maura opened up the paints and began to work. It was a gray and rainy day outside. She wanted to capture it on the canvas with a lot of blues and purples to highlight the shadows in the clouds and in the waves. She brought out highlights with brilliant white paint that lit up the painting despite the grayness of the scene. It took a couple of hours to get the painting to look how she wanted, but she finally did it. She stood back, admiring her work at the end, and then added her initials, "MM," in a beautiful, flowing script. She sighed contentedly. Every stroke, every nuance of color, brought Maura joy when her brush touched the canvas. It was such a relief to pull the images that crowded her head and to place them on paper or canvas. Painting and drawing buoyed her up and brought her a peace she hadn't known existed. It was like active meditation. Sometimes, when she drew or painted, she wasn't really seeing the canvas or paper, and it seemed as though her hand moved of its own accord as it raced to capture the image that hovered in her brain like a ghost. It was a delightful surprise to see it appear beneath her brushes or pencil.

Maura put down her brush briefly and stretched, arching her back and reaching as tall as she could before bending over. She liked doing that, too. She couldn't bend certain ways as a seal. Being a human has some advantages.

Giddy with the completion of the painting, she swooped in and gave Skipper a kiss and a hug. She lay, perfectly content on the couch for a few minutes, thinking about what to do next, her mind whirling with designs.

She wished she didn't have to wait for this painting to dry before starting a new one. Maura wished for a second easel. She would need to ask Rory. He tried to explain the currency to her and how things were bought and sold. She was still extremely confused about it. From what she understood, if she sold her paintings, she would have currency to buy other things, like more art supplies or another easel. She would ask him if this would work when he got home.

Maura remembered Rory asking her to do a watercolor for his mom of one of the sand paintings for the upcoming holiday. She pushed herself up from the couch and went to the desk.

Pulling out a sheet of watercolor paper, she taped it down. Then, she took a pencil and lightly sketched a design. She was glad she had picked up the slipper shells the other day, and had tucked the moon snail shell into her pocket. She set them in front of her, turning them this way and that to see how the light created shadows on the shells.

Next, Maura went to the bathroom to fill a container with water before settling down to paint the sand painting. She worked carefully. She wanted this to be a special painting for Rory's mom, so she added subtle details with a tiny dry brush technique.

She was concentrating so hard that she did not hear Rory come into the house but felt his presence as he stood behind her, peering at her painting.

"That's beautiful," she heard him say when she lifted her brush to rinse it.

"Oh!" She jumped and carefully avoided the wet watercolor. "It's the one for your mom."

Maura stood up and turned to face Rory. He gathered her in his arms, and she heard him murmur in her hair, "She'll love it."

"And I love this," she told him a little huskily. "There's nothing like being in your arms. It's my favorite place to be."

He held her more tightly. They stood like that for several minutes until Skipper approached them and lightly pawed at them. Maura broke away from Rory, laughing. She dropped to her knees and hugged Skipper.

"You wanted a hug too, didn't you, Skipper," she told the dog.

Rory played along and dropped to a knee, "Group hug," he crowed as he put his arm around Maura and Skipper.

Rory took a minute to look at the painting on the easel before commenting, "Maura, this is fantastic. I love the way you captured the passion in the clouds and the depths of the sea. The mist of clouds over the sun trying to peep out at the end of a storm is phenomenal."

Maura blushed, said thank you, and added, "When I sell a few pieces, I want another easel and several more canvases. I'm anxious to start another large painting, but I must wait until this one dries completely."

"Maura, we can get another easel and several canvases to keep you busy," Rory reassured her. "Why don't we go today? Then, you'll have things to work on and can build up a portfolio to share with the galleries. Anyways, I would like to get a nice frame for the painting for Mom, too."

"Today?" Maura asked excitedly. "I would love that, Rory. Let's go, please."

They returned to the arts and crafts store for more supplies. Rory wasn't as frustrated with putting together the second easel. It wasn't long before everything was set up.

"I'll need to get photographing your work, too," Rory said. "We need to record it before it heads out the door to a gallery or the bookstore. We'll want to deliver a few pieces to both this weekend."

Maura moved through the week in a happy rhythm. Rory was caught up in the tensions brewing around the cause of the fire. He had dropped off the blueprints to the fire marshall and was questioned not only by the fire department, but the police as well. They were stoic and not able to give Rory any updates. To keep his mind from wildly speculating too much, he poured some of his energy into teaching Maura how to read and write using the books he picked up at the bookstore. Maura felt she was doing well, particularly with concrete things such as a dog, bed, sea, and sky. It was the sight words that had no meaning to Maura. After breakfast, they both went to work with Rory taking on new projects and Maura painting and drawing. Skipper spent his time going between Rory's office and Maura's drawing room but spent most of his time with Maura on the couch. Rory teased her about stealing his dog.

It was funny, thought Maura. *When Rory is out of the house for any reason, I feel such an emptiness inside. Here, with him working down the hallway, it's as if our energies are on a current in the ocean. We're connected. It's nice.*

When they broke midday, they had lunch, did some lovemaking, or both, and returned to work until evening. Their week went by quickly. Maura thought she had never been so happy.

30

RORY

They had a lazy Saturday morning. Rory loved waking up next to Maura. He woke her with soft kisses and had a languid lovemaking session, settling into one another's arms afterward. Skipper drew them out of bed, and Rory realized how late it was.

"We need to get the paintings and drawings together for the bookstore and gallery this morning, Maura. We need to get up and out. I'll take care of Skipper if you can start breakfast."

Maura yawned and blinked sleepily at him in response. Her smile was small but sultry, and he couldn't be pulled back to bed, not this morning. She pouted a little, realizing his intent, but nodded to his question.

After breakfast, they looked at paintings and drawings to choose when they heard a voice say, 'Hello.' Skipper raced down the stairs.

"It's Lizzie," Rory told Maura. "I told her about your artwork."

"We're up here," he yelled down the stairs. "Come on up, Lizzie."

In a moment, Lizzie's head peeked around the doorway. "Hi," she greeted.

"Hi," Maura and Rory chorused.

"So, this is where the magic happens?" she asked. "Rory told me about your paintings, Maura. I was anxious to see them."

"You came just in time," Rory said, "we're about to head to the gallery and bookstore to drop some off on consignment."

"I'm glad I came when I did," Lizzie returned, entering the room.

Rory noticed that Maura hung back a little from Lizzie. Lizzie had a strong personality and could be formidable in situations. He knew Lizzie liked and appreciated art, so he was sure she would complement Maura's work.

Lizzie studied the paintings and drawings critically. Eventually, in somewhat awe, she turned to Maura and said, "Maura, these are quite amazing. What a talent you have."

Maura blushed and said thank you.

Lizzie went on, "Your attention to detail is amazing. Where did you learn to draw?"

Rory shot Lizzie a look. That was unfair. He had told her Maura was a Selki. He frowned.

Maura answered truthfully, "I don't know. When Rory gave me a pencil, it all started pouring out of me. It started when I was describing the patterns of the sand paintings."

"Yeah, Rory told me they're like beautiful mandalas with natural objects," Lizzie interrupted. "But your art, didn't you learn in school, or maybe from an artistic family member? Did you take some classes at any time?" Lizzie badgered. "Did you see that special program on PBS about Jon Foreman or look at his stuff online?"

Maura looked blankly back at Lizzie's intense stare. She squirmed uncomfortably.

"Lizzie..." Rory said in a warning tone.

"What, bro?" she countered him. "She had to have run across some of this somewhere. I mean her 'sand paintings' on the beach are really similar to Foreman's art. And this natural mandala thing has become pretty popular on social media. I know of a lady in Maryland who claims to commune with fairies. She makes mandalas from leaves, blossoms, and twigs. They're gorgeous."

Maura looked interested. "Really? More people do sand paintings?"

Lizzie nodded. "It's become increasingly popular; that's why it is hard to believe that you just came up with all this out of thin air." She turned to Rory. "Right?"

Rory tried to make things lighter and quipped, "Great minds think alike..." He was annoyed at Lizzie trying to shoot bullets through the reality about Maura. Lizzie was trying to catch Maura in a lie, and he didn't like it at all.

"She says she's never seen anything else like this, and you haven't shown her the examples?"

Rory shrugged and shook his head. Why hadn't he shown Maura examples of land art? He certainly knew about it. He raked his fingers through his hair, feeling guilty.

"I think I would like to see more examples sometime," Maura agreed. "I don't have anything to compare it to. It's just in my head. It's like magic." Maura sounded happy, and even a little wistful.

"Rory or I can share that with you." She added, backing down from her belligerent stance, "But, Maura, I like how you've captured them with graphite and watercolor. It's an interesting way to preserve the fleeting art instead of a photograph."

"We can do that, but right now, Lizzie, I'm sorry, but we need to get these paintings and drawings to the stores. I'm hoping Maura can catch some sales for the upcoming holiday."

"Sure, sure," Lizzie said. "I'm sorry. I just thought I would pop in and check on you. You seemed a little upset yesterday." She eyed him with an intense stare.

Maura looked puzzled and cocked her head, looking at Rory questioningly. He gave his head a little shake in her direction.

"No problem. I appreciate you coming" Rory assured her. "Sorry, we need to go."

"Thank you for your kind words," Maura told Lizzie.

"I'm just being truthful," Lizzie responded and turned to Rory. "Let me help you carry some of these to the car, bro."

Rory nodded and handed her a few things to carry.

"Careful on the steps," he warned.

Maura stayed in the drawing room, still sorting through the paintings.

Downstairs, as they exited and made their way to the car, Rory told Lizzie, "Thanks for not letting Maura know I told you she was a Selki."

Lizzie turned to Rory, saying, "One, she has real talent. Those paintings and drawings are incredible. Two, are you hallucinating? She seems like a real, living human being to me. C'mon Rory, what gives? Where is she really from? I can't imagine that she didn't have some art training.

Maybe she's just not telling you. She's sweet, but is she being truthful, Rory?"

"Well, maybe when you get to know her better, and if she's comfortable with it, she'll let you see her sealskin."

"Humph, that would be something," Lizzie agreed but added acerbically, "and you're becoming the king of fantasyland." She helped Rory stack the artwork carefully in the car. After she hugged him and said, "See ya, bro."

Rory watched her go.

31

MAURA

aura wasn't sure what to make of Lizzie. She had been very kind in her compliments but seemed to be probing for something untrue. She wondered if Rory told Lizzie she was a Selki. But she didn't ask those kinds of questions. Today, though, she didn't have time to mull over why or why not. They had to get to the gallery and bookstore. She went downstairs to Rory.

The bookstore was busy with holiday shoppers. Jazzlynn was delighted to take the paintings. Rory had been in contact with her and discussed pricing. Jazzlynn thought they would sell this weekend and asked Rory to be on standby to bring more.

"I'll let you know tomorrow afternoon, all right?"

They agreed. Rory also shared the watercolor of the sand painting Maura created for his mom and also the large seascape.

"Oooh! These are lovely!" Jazzlynn gushed. "I wish I had time to run to your car to look at the larger acrylics, but my assistant is on break."

Indeed, a line formed behind them. Maura and Rory retreated to let Jazzlynn sell her wares. She showed the paintings and drawings to the people coming up to the register, nodding who the artist was in Maura's retreating form.

The next stop was the gallery. Elizabeth, too, was delighted to take on the paintings. She loved the large seascape and was in awe of the underwater scene.

"Are you a diver?" she asked Maura.

"In a way," Maura answered, smiling. "It's a beautiful world under the surface."

"It certainly is," Elizabeth agreed. "We have an open house tomorrow if you want to drop by. Let's say we'll set up a formal opening for you in the spring. Maybe we'll catch the Mother's Day crowd on the first weekend of May?"

"That sounds great, Elizabeth," Rory answered for them.

When they left, Rory asked Maura if she wanted to attend the open house tomorrow. Maura shrugged. She didn't know what it entailed.

"Tell me more about this Open House thing," Maura questioned Rory.

He explained that it was a great way to showcase art and that people liked to come and socialize as well.

"You would be meeting and talking with a lot of strangers," he warned.

"But, if they came to see and enjoy the art, wouldn't they be more like a kindred spirit? I think it would be easier to talk with them."

"We'll have to get you a dress and shoes," he suggested. "I might want to call Lizzie for help with this. I don't have a clue."

Maura didn't like the idea of calling Lizzie for help. In a small voice, she shrugged and said, 'Okay. '

Rory called Lizzie from the car, asking for her help. "I'm thinking just the department stores, not the entire mall," Rory requested. "It's going to be crazy enough with holiday shoppers."

You could almost hear Lizzie make a face. "A dress?" she asked. I'm not good at dresses, but Jo is. Is it okay if she comes along?"

"Sure, sure," Rory agreed, "as long as we can take you out after shopping to thank you."

"That would be fine," Lizzie said. "Meet you at the mall in twenty."

Rory stepped on the gas to get to the local mall. It was full of holiday shoppers, and they had to park nearly at the end of the parking lot. The wind was blowing, and it was chilly. Rory put his arm around Maura to guide her into the store.

At the entrance to the department store, all Maura could see were bright red bows and lots of baubles that looked like iridescent bubbles on the sea. There were fake trees crusted with ornaments and ribbons. Maura couldn't imagine it being able to breathe if it were a real tree.

"Why do they do that to the trees?" Maura asked. "Do they do it to real ones?"

"Sure," Rory said, "It's part of the holiday tradition to decorate the trees."

"Real ones?" she asked.

"Yes," Rory told her. "Do you want to get a tree? I hadn't even thought of it."

"I don't want to do that to a tree; it wouldn't be able to breathe," Maura said.

Rory barked a laugh and then apologized. "I'm sorry," he apologized to Maura. "I didn't mean to laugh at you."

Maura looked annoyed, and Rory apologized. Truthfully, Maura was overwhelmed by the holiday glitz. The store was overbright and overwhelming, and she was dreading this experience.

And then Lizzie and her wife came in. Maura was surprised when she met Jo. She was the complete antithesis of Lizzie. She was petite, too, with long, blond, curling hair that was feminine and styled. She shook Maura's hand.

"This is exciting," she said after introductions. "I love to shop."

Lizzie rolled her eyes at her wife. "I know," she replied sarcastically.

They made their way to the formal clothes at the back of the store. Maura's mouth hung open as she passed through the different departments. Rory had to pull her along as Jo was chatting up a storm and getting ahead of them.

"What color are you looking for?" she asked Maura. "What size are you? What's the event?"

Thankfully, Rory explained the gallery's last-minute invitation to an open house. He explained that they had just taken several of Maura's pieces.

"Color?" Maura said. "Maybe brown?"

"Or maybe blues," Lizzie suggested, "since you have drawn and painted several scenes about the ocean."

Maura looked at her with renewed interest. "That sounds great."

"Except a lot of ocean-themed prints are summer-oriented. This is December. And, since it's tomorrow, you don't have time to have anything custom-made. But, let's look." As an aside, she continued, "If you can't find something here, I would suggest a bridal salon. The mall is insane with holiday shoppers. How formal do you want to be?"

Maura shrugged. "I don't know. This is my first gallery open house."

"Maura lived in a pretty isolated area of New Brunswick," Rory explained.

"I'll say," Lizzie commented and then looked guilty. "From what Rory told me. An island?" she asked Maura.

"Yes, a remote island," Maura said. She began to wonder how much Rory had told Lizzie about her. He seemed distracted and uncomfortable with the women's clothes, and his hands were stuffed in his pockets.

"Since you're petite," Jo suggested, "you should probably look for a long dress and then wear a little bit of a heel for shoes."

She started sifting through the clothes on the rack. "Here's a pretty brown one," she said as she pulled out a long dress with velvet gores. "It's pretty, but it's just 'okay' I think. It's not a 'wowza' kind of dress."

Maura thought it was very pretty. The velvet looked like seal fur. She kept touching it.

"And this one is incredibly sexy," Lizzie said, pulling out a shiny dress with very large starfish. I think it would be like a second skin."

Rory looked interested in this.

"Ugh!" Jo cried. "Most of these are ghastly. When you're petite, you can't wear a lot of ruffles and bows. You need something straightforward."

Maura had taken some interest now and was going through the racks. She found a dress and gasped. She pulled it out. It was tea-length velvet with filmy chiffon sleeves. Swirling appliques covered the bodice area, looking like ocean waves.

"How about this one?" she asked the group.

"Oooh! Gorgeous," Jo agreed. "Let's have you try it on."

Jo herded Maura to a changing room. Maura gave a slightly panicked look to Rory, but he motioned her to go on.

"She'll need lingerie and shoes to go with that," Lizzie suggested to Rory.

He nodded. "Maybe Jo can help her with the feminine stuff."

"Oh, she would be happy to do that," Lizzie laughed. "Look at her already, taking on Maura. You'll have her dressed from top to toe before Jo is through. She's having a blast."

"I'm not sure what Maura thinks," Rory said. "She looked a little scared."

Lizzie laughed again. "Jo can be a little scary with stuff like this. But, she's kind. Maura will be fine," she reassured him.

Jo led Maura from the dressing room. "What do you think?" she asked.

Maura noticed Rory's reaction. His eyes dilated, and he had that smile on him as though he wanted to mate with her right there, in the store. This pleased her, but she wasn't sure if she should be shy or coy. Maura liked Rory's reaction but felt very exposed in the dress. She had only been wearing comfortable sweatpants, sweatshirts, and leggings. She wasn't used to the human clothes. It was difficult to think she would wear this dress around other humans. Jo was so nice and knowledgeable. She was also a little bossy. She was telling Rory and Lizzie to go away. She said she would help Maura with lingerie and shoes.

"And," she said, turning to Maura, "if it's all right with you, I'll pick you up, and we'll get your fingernails and toes done, and I can do your make-up and hair?"

Fingers and toes done? Maura panicked. What did she mean? She looked at her fingers and toes.

Lizzie jumped in. "She means decorating your fingernails and toenails, Maura," Lizzie explained. "Show her, Jo."

Jo stretched out her hand to show her nails decorated for the holidays. Maura looked at Rory.

He shrugged as if to say, "Go ahead if you want to."

Rory and Lizzie left for other shopping with the promise they would meet later for drinks.

Maura let herself be herded around the store to find the other necessary items to wear to tomorrow's gallery open house. It seemed like a lot of work, but Jo kept reassuring her that it was all necessary. But was it necessary? As a seal, she was just a seal. Other seals and Selkis accepted her for herself. She didn't have to put on anything or remove anything to share herself. She was just Maura, and everyone accepted that. On the other hand, humans seemed to want to put on a fake personality or change themselves somehow, at least sometimes, for other humans. Maura wracked her brain to think of an ocean creature that did this. Octopi and others used camouflage, but this was different. There were different expectations. Jo seemed to know all about it but also kept her own personality. Maura admired that.

32

RORY

*R*ory wondered what he was getting into with Jo taking over Maura's outfit for the gallery opening as he handed over his credit card. Maura was still looking a little uncomfortable. Her expression was pleading, but she had also caught some of Jo's enthusiasm for the event.

He did wonder if they were taking it a bit too far with the formal dress and shoes. Lizzie grabbed his arm.

"You owe me," she told him.

"What?" he asked Lizzie.

"You owe me for having Jo as my wife and for allowing her to help Maura with this feminine stuff."

"Did you tell Jo that Maura was a Selki?" Rory wanted to know.

"Nope. All she knows is that Maura is from some remote part of Canada. When you're ready to tell her, you can. Don't put that on me. C'mon, let's do some Christmas shopping," Lizzie suggested, "and maybe I can talk you into buying me a brew."

Rory made a face as they moved from the department store to the overcrowded mall. Christmas music blared as the crowds moved in hoards in and out of stores.

"Where did you want to shop?" Rory had almost to yell to get Lizzie to hear him.

She shrugged, and that didn't help the situation. Suddenly, Lizzie pulled him into a store.

"Look at that!" she said and pointed to a necklace. That would match the dress Maura had been wearing picked out." The necklace was simple and elegant with its ripple of silver and enameled teals and blues and spoke of a wave on the sea.

"It is beautiful," Rory agreed with Lizzie.

And only a moment later, an older, platinum-blonde woman with heavy make-up came over to them, asking if they needed assistance. Lizzie didn't hesitate. She pointed to the necklace.

"This is a *gorgeous* piece," the saleslady said, emphasizing gorgeous as she unlocked the case. A legendary Scottish jewelry artisan created it. Her work is stunning and sometimes difficult to get in the United States." She held it out for Rory and Lizzie to examine.

"C'mon, Rory. You said she was 'the one.' Buy it!" Lizzie urged. "And it's her first gallery event."

"Okay, okay," Rory acquiesced. "This gallery event is setting me back a lot," he complained. "And Jo and Maura still need to do the hair, nails, and make-up tomorrow."

"Aren't we lucky to have two such gorgeous, feminine ladies to love," Lizzie quipped, putting an arm around Rory's shoulders.

"We'll take it," he said to the saleslady, "and can you please wrap it?"

"Certainly, sir," she said, taking his credit card and the necklace to the rear counter to process the transaction and wrap the gift.

Lizzie checked the time," We need to meet the girls soon at the pub."

"I'm ready for a brew," Rory said. "Get me out of this mall."

They were having a beer when Maura and Jo entered the restaurant carrying several bags. Maura looked different. Rory always thought she was beautiful, but someone had applied make-up artfully, bringing out her large eyes. Her mouth was a rosy red. He wanted to bite and kiss those lips.

Jo interrupted his thoughts by handing him his credit card and a handful of receipts.

"Wow," Lizzie commented.

He paled at the handful of receipts she put in his hand.

"Hi," he greeted Maura, "You look gorgeous!"

"Just wait until tomorrow," Jo warned. "I have plans."

Lizzie rolled her eyes at this. "Oh, boy," was all she said.

Jo grinned at her.

They settled into their booth. Rory put his arm around Maura. "How are you doing?" he whispered in her ear.

She turned to him and smiled, "Good," she replied, "really good, actually. Jo's been amazing and teaching me so much."

"Good," Rory agreed, "And Lizzie and I found something to go along with your dress."

He pulled the small, wrapped box from his coat pocket and put it before Maura.

Her eyes widened.

"Open it!" Lizzie urged.

Maura did. She teared up when she saw the beautiful blue wave pendant in heavy silver.

"Oh, Rory. It's one of the most beautiful things I've ever seen," she told him softly. "Thank you."

She leaned over and kissed him. He kissed her back and tried very hard not to deepen the kiss and kiss her more. He was suddenly hungry for her.

"Let's eat dinner and go home," he whispered.

She caught the lustful glint in his eye and nodded.

The waitress approached the table and asked if Maura and Jo wanted drinks. Maura looked at Rory.

"Maybe something lighter than a Bloody Caesar this time?" he asked her.

She nodded her head vigorously.

"What about a hard cider?" Jo suggested. "They serve ones from the local Cidery here."

"Then you order," Maura urged, "you haven't steered me wrong yet," she told Jo.

"And you can order dinner for me," Maura told Rory.

"Their fish and chips are excellent here," Lizzie suggested.

"That sounds great to me. We'll both have that," Rory agreed.

Rory relaxed and wasn't worried Maura would make an odd faux pas. They enjoyed themselves but exited after dinner, Rory using Skipper as an excuse. He held Maura's hand as he walked back to the car.

At home, he let Skipper out while Maura put the packages away. Once Skipper was back inside, he took the steps two at a time to reach Maura. When he reached the door to the bedroom, he stopped and stared. Maura was standing, rather shyly, in sexy black lingerie and small, strappy, heeled sandals.

"Wow," he said breathlessly. "Maura..." he trailed off and went to her, holding her gingerly as if she might break.

"Jo thought you would like this outfit," she whispered in his ear.

"She was correct." His voice was husky.

He held her at arm's length, swooped her up in his arms, and carried her to the bed.

"Oh! Oh!" Maura cried out involuntarily.

He wanted to rip the lingerie off, but instead, he took his time kissing and using his tongue to outline the edges of the skimpy pieces. Maura's skin had goosebumps, and she writhed beneath him.

"Keep still," he growled, but not unkindly.

"I can't," she panted. "I want you. I want to mate with you now!"

"Be patient," he told her as he slowly removed the lingerie. He inserted a finger in her. She was so wet and so ready for him. Then he inserted two and reached for her G-spot. She cried out, but he continued and licked at her clitoris until she nearly leaped off the bed. She orgasmed beautifully, not once but two times. It was then he entered her extremely slowly.

"Oh, please, Rory," she begged. "I want you inside of me. Please."

He obliged.

33

MAURA

The aftershocks of orgasm stayed with Maura well through the morning. Her limbs felt liquid. She was almost sad to go with Jo as she wanted to stay at home and in bed with Rory. He kept pulling her to him this morning, squeezing her buttocks when they kissed. She could feel him start stiffening, and she wanted to climb onto him.

Later, she told herself, later. If the lovemaking they had last night was due to her getting primped and wearing skimpy lingerie, she was all for going to the salon for her nails and to have her hair and make-up done. Rory liked the result. She liked how he reacted. Maura wanted to experience more orgasms like she had last night. She was already getting wet at the thought, and there wasn't time to pleasure herself. Rory seemed to like to watch her do that. Maybe after the gallery event, when they returned home, she would play with herself and then try sitting on top of his erect penis. They hadn't tried that yet, and she liked the thought of it. At this point, she couldn't imagine mating with a seal. With Rory, they could play and experiment in endless ways. Each one seemed to be more pleasurable. She liked the human way of mating. No, she loved it and wanted Rory more and more.

Jo picked her up, and she kissed Rory goodbye with a kiss that promised more later. His eyes widened.

Jo instructed Maura to get all of her things for the event.

"You," she ordered Rory, "will meet us there promptly at four."

"Yes, ma'am," Rory replied, saluting Jo.

Jo laughed gaily. "Can't wait!"

Jo introduced Maura to get her nails and toes manicured and her eyebrows waxed and plucked. She also talked Maura into getting waxed...*down there*. Jo called it a 'bikini wax.'

At first, Maura was shocked. Lose her fur? She couldn't imagine it. Jo told her how much Rory would enjoy her smooth, baby-soft skin. She also whispered to Maura how, if she waxed her private area, her orgasms would multiply. But giving up what she coined as her fur made Maura realize she was giving up more of her seal self. Was she ready for this? Jo had been teaching her so many things about being a human female. It was fun, but it was exhausting. Is this what she wanted for the rest of her days? There was so much to remember and to do to maintain what Jo referred to as normal maintenance for a human female. Wistfully, she thought about swimming freely in the ocean. Was she ready to give this up? For Rory? For herself? But, on the other hand, she wanted to please Rory too. He had done so much for her. Giving up her 'fur' was a small thing in return for all he had done. And, according to Jo, she would experience greater pleasure when they mated. It was hard to imagine, but that was something Maura couldn't pass up. That was something for herself. She agreed to the bikini wax. It was painful and brought tears to her eyes, but she persevered. Her newly bare skin seemed foreign to her. It was almost as soft and resilient as a dolphin's skin or the skin of a stingray. She closed her eyes a moment and imagined Rory's look of awe and delight when he discovered what she'd done.

After that experience, Jo took her to another salon for her hair. The woman trimmed her hair and pulled into an updo accented with an exquisite crystal starfish hair accessory. The last thing was to go to Jo and Lizzie's for a make-up tutorial and to dress for the event.

Maura, Lizzie, and Jo arrived at the open house at the gallery as early dusk was falling. The old house that housed the gallery was outlined in white lights. From the outside, Maura could see people milling about. It seemed as crowded as the mall yesterday. She wondered if Rory was there. She wasn't very good at discerning different cars yet. Lizzie and Jo motioned her forward, and she teetered on her high heels.

"Come on," Jo urged, "You look fantastic."

Inside, the crowd glittered in their holiday finery. Elizabeth approached her, tall and elegant in a long winter-white silk dress. She seemed to sparkle with gold and diamonds on her ears, throat, wrists, and hands.

"Maura!" she cried. "Welcome! I'm so glad you could make it this evening. I've been talking about your paintings to many people. Come. Come and meet some of them."

Elizabeth took her elbow and guided her through the crowd, smiling and greeting people on the way. Maura looked wildly around, looking for Rory, Jo, or Lizzie. The crowd swallowed Lizzie and Jo, and Rory was nowhere to be seen.

Elizabeth stopped and introduced her to numerous people, stating, "This is Maura Muir, one of our newest artists. Her paintings capture the essence of the ocean. You can find them over there," she pointed to a spot where she had hung Maura's work.

Everyone was polite and complimentary. Maura smiled and said hello and thank you to more people than she could count. Finally, Elizabeth was distracted by a question and released her elbow.

"Have fun," she whispered to Maura before she smiled and moved to another group of people.

The gallery crowd was like a writhing school of fish. Maura wasn't sure which way to go. She backed against a wall, nearly knocking over a sculpture. The crowd parted a little, and there he was. Her heart swelled with relief and happiness at seeing Rory. He looked so handsome. When their eyes met, it was like a lifeline to Maura. His look reeled her into him.

"Maura, you look beautiful," he told her when he reached her.

"Thank you," she said, somewhat shyly.

He took her hand and said, "Come on, we must celebrate. Even though this isn't an opening dedicated to your paintings, it's a great segue for future shows. There are many people here and look at the crowd around your work.

There was indeed a crowd near her paintings. Maura wasn't sure how to feel. She was happy people liked her paintings, but she also felt very unprotected. Each painting held a part of her heart and soul. When people viewed them, they shared part of her.

Elizabeth was gushing about Maura's work and spied them. "There she is! This is Maura, the artist of these fantastic pieces."

When eyes turned on Maura, she felt completely exposed. However, Rory put an arm around her and steadied her. She wavered, but he held her.

Elizabeth noticed and turned the crowd back to her, saying, "Maura will have her own show soon. We'll call it 'The Essence of the Ocean.' It fits, don't you think?" She asked the small crowd. "Now over here," she went on, leading the others away.

Maura noticed there were small stickers on four of her six paintings.

"What does that mean?" Maura asked Rory.

"It means you've sold four out of six paintings," Rory told her. "Congratulations, Maura! Elizabeth will be wanting more. You'll need to get busy. We might need to buy you another easel."

Maura beamed at this comment. "I would love that."

He grinned and led her to a room where refreshments were set up. Rory pointed out some of the foods displayed and suggested some Maura might like. He also handed her a glass filled with a bubbly liquid and told her it was champagne.

"Oh!" Maura cried in surprise when she took a sip, and the bubbles tickled her nose. She took another sip and savored the flavor. "This is like the nectar of the gods," she told Rory. "It's delicious."

Rory chuckled. "Nectar of the gods? Some people think so. I prefer a good beer, myself."

"Mmm, I don't think I could ever get enough," and sipped some more.

34

RORY

Rory was pleased the evening was such a success for Maura. Lizzie and Jo found them and all toasted Maura for her success. He could barely believe this beautiful, talented woman—no, beautiful, talented Selki—wanted to be with him. And she became more human every day. It surprised him. It pleased him, but part of him was wistful for the shy creature he first met. He knew he wanted to be with her every possible second. He knew he wanted to grow old and watch a million sunrises with her from their living room or the deck.

He was excited for Maura that her paintings were a success. He would need to get her website up and soon. Her success thrilled him.

Now, he was anxious to take Maura home. He wanted her out of her pretty dress and all to himself. He put an arm around her and whispered, "Home soon?" She leaned into him and nodded.

"Yes, please," she told him. "We can use Skipper as an excuse."

"Good idea," he agreed.

They said their thanks and made their goodbyes. Rory tucked Maura into the car. He touched her leg, running it up and down her silky, smooth skin. Touching her bare skin caused him to stiffen and twitch. She squirmed a little in her seat, and he knew what that meant. She was wet and ready for him.

Skipper was anxious to see them, and his needs delayed Rory's plans. They took Skipper outside, and for once, he wanted to run and play in the yard instead of coming in quickly at night. Rory sighed. He threw the ball a few times while Maura prepped Skipper's food and refreshed his water.

"Come on, boy," he told the dog. "We need to go inside."

Maura was in the kitchen. She had removed her heels. She looked weary.

"Are you all right?" he asked her.

She smiled. "Sure. I'm just a little tired after tonight's excitement. And these shoes! How do women wear them all the time? I saw so many varieties when we were at the store. Barefoot is definitely better."

"I'm sure a lot of women would agree with you. But there are advantages to high heels. They make you taller, and they look incredibly sexy," he said. "Just seeing them on you makes me excited."

"Really," Maura commented. "I had no idea. Men are odd."

"We are an odd lot," he chuckled. "And I fantasize about you wearing heels only. Well, that, and maybe a little lingerie."

"If you can help me with this dress, I can make that fantasy come true," she said coyly.

"Let's go up to the bedroom," he suggested.

Getting the dress off was a challenge with zippers and hooks, the tulle underskirt, and chiffon sleeves. Rory needed to be very careful. Maura was extremely patient. She wore a small smile, and he thought it was in anticipation of their lovemaking, but it looked like she had a secret.

The time taking the dress off was worth the wait. Like a model, she stood in a lace bustier and what could laughingly be called underwear. It was a bit of lace, a butterfly covering her clitoris, and that was about it, along with string. He stared. Something was different. Maura had been waxed and she was silky smooth in her private area.

He wanted her so badly. He wanted to take her immediately, shoving himself into her. On the other hand, he wanted to explore every millimeter of her newly bare skin. And she knew it. The newly feminine ways Jo introduced her to had given her confidence he hadn't yet seen in Maura.

"I need to see this and to touch you," he told Maura, his voice husky with anticipation.

"Go ahead," Maura permitted him.

He peeled the tiny panties from her and just stared for a moment or two before he asked her to lie down where he could begin touching with his fingers and his tongue. She was so wet and so ready, but he wanted to prolong this. The waxing left her sensitive, and she orgasmed easily, over and over, crying out his name and crying out to Sedna.

Maura put a hand on his face and asked him to stop. He pulled away, surprised.

"What's wrong?" he asked.

"I want you on your back now," she requested.

He complied as she sat on top of him, lowering herself bit by bit on his very hard, thick shaft. She cried out when he was fully inside of her, and she rocked back and forth, and he thrust into her, raising his hips.

He loved watching her face alight with passion. He begged her, this time, to lower her breasts to his mouth so that he could nibble and suck. They tantalized him as they swung, heavy like ripe fruit for the picking. When she did, he began to lose control himself. She screamed in orgasm again, and he came too, crying out her name.

Maura collapsed on top of him, and he held her tightly.

"I liked that," she whispered.

"Me too," he agreed.

"Soon," she insisted. "I want more soon."

"I will comply as soon as I can," he promised, hoping he wasn't too spent to comply with her wishes.

She rolled off of him and curled up against him. They dozed for a few hours and then made love again.

The phone ringing brought them out of a hazy sleep. Rory answered, disentangling himself from Maura to take the call.

Lizzie's voice was teasing, booming in his ear, "Good morning! I hope I didn't wake you too early."

Rory grunted in response, and Lizzie laughed.

"Apparently, Maura is Jo's new protégé. She wants to take Maura to one of those big beauty stores where there's tons of make-up, a salon, and stuff. She wants to take Maura to brunch too."

By this time, Maura was awake and looked quizzically at Rory. He relayed the proposed plan to Maura.

Maura's response was a gasp of delight and a crowing of "Yes! That would be so much fun!"

Lizzie heard the answer through the phone and laughed.

Acerbically, Rory stated, "I think Jo has warped Maura, Lizzie. My credit cards will never be the same."

"No worries, Rory," Lizzie chuckled, "after last night's little soiree, I think you have an up-and-coming artist on Long Island. Maura will be getting her own credit card soon. Her paintings were selling like hotcakes."

35

MAURA

The time with Jo was incredibly fun. Jo reminded Maura of her youngest sister, Rhona. She was bright and vivacious, telling Maura they had to 'find their fun' to make things worthwhile. Maura loved her positivity and told her so. Friendship was something new to Maura and she found she liked it.

They had a blast at the beauty store, exploring every inch, laughing, talking, and commenting positively and negatively about some of the makeup choices. This time with Jo was so different from her times with Rory, and she loved it, too. The choices humans had were immeasurable. The opportunities were so vast. It was a little overwhelming, but she enjoyed exploring the world as a human. She couldn't imagine going back to being a seal after learning the wonders she was experiencing as a human.

As a seal, her choices were minimal. Sure, she had fun, but her days focused on survival—staying away from sharks, nets, and boat rudders. Finding food daily was paramount, as was finding a safe place to haul out.

On their way home, Jo decided to drop Maura off and then go get pizza for the crew.

"Will you go in and let them know? Lizzie or Rory can text me if they want anything beyond our usual order," Jo asked her.

"Sure," Maura agreed. "Not a problem."

She let herself into the house. It was pretty quiet. She listened and thought she heard voices and went to investigate. She thought Lizzie and Rory might be in Rory's office, or perhaps Lizzie wanted to see the paintings again. She went up the stairs, listening so she would know where they were. They were in the drawing room.

"It's in here, I think," she heard Rory say.

And then, Maura heard a door open and a gasp from Lizzie with a stage whisper of, "Oh. My. God."

Maura's heart plummeted. Was Rory showing Lizzie her pelt? He had no right to do that! Didn't Rory realize that her pelt was hers and was private? It was like a stranger seeing her naked. Her pelt wasn't like a piece of clothing in the store to have on view for everyone to see and touch. It was *her* pelt. It was hers alone to decide when and who to share it with. She felt she had been exposed, laid bare for Lizzie to see. That wasn't Rory's choice. It was hers. Anger flared within her. She stepped into the room. There they were, crouching at the closet door, staring inside. Lizzie held out her hand to touch the whiskers on the face.

"What do you think you are doing?" she asked, her anger billowing to the surface.

Rory looked up, with a guilty look suddenly on his face.

"I'm sorry, Maura, I didn't think you would mind," he said haltingly.

"I do mind. This is private and it's my choice who is able to see that I am a Selki. You've betrayed me, Rory. This is like raping me publicly. Give me that!" she reached and grabbed the pelt, hugging it to herself.

Rory and Lizzie stepped back, staring at her, shocked at her violent reaction.

She turned and ran down the stairs, tears blinding her. How could he do that? She raced out the door and down the stairs to the beach. Rory's voice could be heard plaintively calling, "Maura! Wait! I'm sorry!" and Lizzie yelling apologies too.

Maura didn't care. She had been betrayed, and suddenly, she hated humans. Being a seal was so much easier. She stripped her clothes off and stepped into her pelt. It felt like coming home after a long, long time. She waddled into the water and dove into the cold December sea to swim as far away and fast as she could from Rory and Lizzie.

36

RORY

Rory was stunned into silence by Maura's anger. They had never discussed that her pelt was private. He knew they had to keep her being a Selki a secret, but he thought Lizzie was a safe person to share the secret. He was wrong. Maura definitely thought it was wrong.

When Maura ran out of the house, it took him a minute to realize what she was doing. Skipper didn't run after her. He sat on the couch and howled like Rory had never heard before. The howl spurned him on.

"Maura!" he shouted. "Wait! I'm sorry. I'm sorry! Maura, come back!" he screamed, but the winter wind tore away his words.

He watched her seal form dive into the water and disappear. He sank on the steps, not knowing what to do. He had lost her—just like that— over something incredibly stupid. He kept staring at the ocean. Lizzie came up behind him and then sat.

"She really is a Selki," she said in disbelief.

Jo's voice called from the top of the stairs. "Hey guys, pizza's here. What are you two doing? Did you see that seal? Was it on your beach, Rory?"

They turned and looked up at Jo. Rory had tears streaming from his face.

"What's wrong, Rory?" Jo asked. "Where's Maura?"

Lizzie pointed to the ocean. Jo came slowly down the steps and sat on the step above them. Rory couldn't talk. His voice was thick with tears and sorrow.

"Please, Lizzie," he choked out. "You tell her."

And Lizzie did. She explained to Jo that Maura was a Selki and they had just seen Maura as a seal.

They all sat, watching the sea for a long, long time. The pizza was forgotten. Rory would have sat all day and all night, but Lizzie finally cajoled him to go inside.

When they got inside, they were all shivering. Jo poured them shots of whiskey, and the burning fire of the liquid warmed their insides a little. She turned on the oven to heat up the ice-cold pizza. Skipper lay by the back door, whining softly as if he was crying too.

"Rory, I'm sorry," Lizzie apologized. "I shouldn't have asked you to show me her pelt."

Rory shook his head. "Not your fault. I had no idea she was so sensitive about it. It's been part of our lives since I found her on the beach. It's part of her. I..." he couldn't go on as unshed tears choked him again. Finally, he looked miserably at Lizzie and Jo. "Do you think she'll come back?"

Lizzie slung an arm around Rory and gave him a one-armed hug Her eyes were filled with sadness and guilt. "No idea, bro. I hope so, for your sake. I know you love her deeply."

He nodded. "This is going to sound smarmy, but I don't think I can live without her. Her leaving is tearing out a piece of my soul. It's like all those love songs. They finally have meaning now."

Jo put an arm around him and patted him on the back. She took Lizzie's hand with her other hand and squeezed tightly. "I know what you mean," she told Rory. "But Maura loves you. And you know that old saying that if you love something, you must let it go and be free. Maybe that's what you have to do with Selkis, too. After all, she's part wild animal. Seals are beautiful, but they are wild and dangerous creatures."

Rory's shoulders slumped. He went to the couch and looked out over the ocean, wondering where Maura was.

"Do you think I've pushed her too much into being human? I just wanted her to be happy in the human world. She seemed happy. Her art made her happy. Skipper made her happy. I thought I made her happy. I don't know anymore. Maybe I didn't give her a chance to tell me what she really wanted. Maybe I am being selfish."

"Stop beating yourself up, Rory. Listen to what Jo said. She said to let her go. It's like that saying of 'trusting the Universe' and everything the gurus say about letting go. It sounds like a lot of bunk, but it's true. Think about it, Rory. Let her go. I'm hoping she will return, but you need to trust what's best and the Universe," Lizzie suggested gently.

37

MAURA

Maura swam as swiftly as she could, torpedoing through the water. How could Rory betray her like that? It was her choice who she could tell or not tell that she was a Selki. Humans had a difficult time knowing that she was a seal and a human woman. How could she have thought that he loved her? How could she have been so stupid? She had been raised by women who drummed into her that human men duped Selkis all the time. The men were not to be trusted. Rory had hurt her deeply, by sharing her secret without telling her. How could she ever trust him again? She doubted his love for her. She doubted everything right now.

She stopped swimming and went up to the surface. She was miles from the coast and Rory's house. She could see a dot on shore to what she thought was his house if she squinted. She stared at it, wondering about Rory. And then she looked around. The sea was all around her. And although filled with life, she was virtually an island. There was no one, no creature that loved and cared for her in this cold water.

She dove again into the kelp forest, letting the strands of kelp caress her. The kelp glided over her wet pelt, but it wasn't the same as Rory's touch. His touch sent ripples of pleasure through her, something she hadn't experienced as a seal. The kelp forest reminded her of her sisters. They had many happy hours playing hide and seek in the kelp and swimming as though they were dancing, pretending the kelp were long, beautiful scarves and what they imagined human dresses looked like. Her sisters. She had no idea where Rhona was. But Kelsi, she was south of her in New Jersey. She wondered if she could make it there and swam to the surface to get her bearings.

South. She started to swim. She wasn't with the herd this time. She was alone again. It didn't used to bother her, but now, she missed Rory. Maura stopped swimming. Her head bobbed at the surface. There was water all around her and no other creature in sight. The ocean was so vast. Even though it was filled with millions of creatures, it could be a very lonely place. She thought of the places Rory had taken her and thought being on land could be the same.

She was lonely. She wanted to be with Rory and not alone in this vast sea. She wouldn't mind seeing the herd again but didn't want to mate with another seal. She only wanted to mate with Rory.

Perhaps he had inadvertently shown her pelt. How could she be angry with that? Perhaps she had overreacted. She missed him. If she went back to him, could she be happy as a human? Would she need to give up being a seal forever? Was it worth it? Was Rory worth it? Rory was teaching her how to be independent, and independent woman in human society. That was a gift. The learning was a burden she would need to bear. She dove again, swimming down to the kelp and letting the fronds wrap around her like a hug. Maura was so torn in her decision. Stay in the sea and stay a seal, or return to Rory and live like a human. A dark shape loomed above her, blotting out the sun that showed dully through the water. Shark! She shuddered and swam further into the kelp, hiding. She hated sharks. The shark swam above her lazily, as if patrolling the water, knowing its power to hunt and kill.

And that's an easy way out. To give herself to the shark, and the decision would be made. No other angst. Is that what she wanted? The shark swam closer and closer. Maura waited. She could see its dead, black eyes as it scanned for food. And, it spotted her. Maura swam as fast as she could – swimming because her life depended on it. Those hateful dead eyes. The shark's jaws snapped. No, she didn't want to be shark food. She wanted Rory. She swam faster and faster, torpedoing through the kelp until the shark gave up.

She hid among the fronds again, eyes scanning for the shark, hoping it had swum away, seeking other prey. Her racing heart began to slow back to a normal beat. And Maura realized this was not the life she wanted. She wanted to be with Rory and not fight for survival daily in the ocean. She made her way to the surface to see where she was and to get her bearings.

She was going back to Rory. She hoped he wouldn't be angry with her. She needed to know that he loved her not only as a human but also as a Selki.

She arrived at his beach. Darkness was gathering. Lights were on in his house. She heard Skipper howl. It was a sound she had never heard before. It sounded mournful.

She stripped from her pelt and held it over one arm as she slowly climbed the stairs. She heard Skipper again. This time, he was pawing and scratching at the door, barking and barking.

"What is it, boy?" she heard Rory's voice. "What's going on?"

When the door opened, she reached the top of the stairs. Skipper raced out to greet her, but Rory did not. He stood. His body was in a halo of warm light from the inside. But his hesitation lasted only a moment. He was running towards her, catching her in his arms, kissing her, and telling her he loved her.

Maura let him hold her and melted into his arms, her pelt dropping onto the sand and grass. She put her arms around him and held onto him as tightly as possible. If she could have, she would have melded to his body.

"I'm so sorry, Maura. I was thoughtless," he apologized, speaking into her hair and ear.

Maura knew this was a moment of decision for her. She needed to make him understand, be sure he loved her, and let Rory know who she was as much as she loved him.

"The sea pulls me," she admitted, "and I always will be a Selki. I'm a creature of Sedna. I'm part seal." Maura hesitated for a long moment and turned, staring out at the water.

She saw the doubt in his eyes and the hurt. He must think she wanted to return to the sea.

She heard Rory say, "But I love you."

"What comes after 'I love you?'" Maura asked, turning to him again and searching his face for answers.

"Life," he stated succinctly, looking into her eyes. "My life. Your life. Our lives together. You are my tomorrow."

Rory kissed her gently.

"You are why I can't return to the sea forever. I want to be with *you* forever," Maura told him. "I love you, but you must know and understand that I may need to be with the sea sometimes. Not long, but it is part of me, and I am part of it as much as I am part of you."

Rory gathered Maura in his arms. He could live with that. Skipper leaped around them joyfully. Maura opened her arm, and he wriggled between them and licked their faces until they both doubled over in laughter.

They both turned then, holding hands, watching the interplay of light sparkling on the water as the sun set, feeling the joy of being and the joy of being together.

The End

ABOUT THE AUTHOR

Sharon, born in 1959, grew up in central Pennsylvania, surrounded by beautiful mountains. Writing has been a lifelong passion. For Sharon, writing is like breathing. She says she has more stories in her head to write down than lifetimes to live. Sharon is a national award-winning author, librarian, and the author of several educational publications. She is also an avid gardener and jewelry artist.

www.sharon-brubaker.com